A PLACE IN TIME

THE SPIRIT OF PETERBOROUGH
Book: 1

TOM GOYMOUR

*A tale of fiction linked to the historical
documented ghostly past!*

❀ ❀ ❀ ❀ ❀

ISBN: 9798429083810

CONTENTS

Prologue

It was dark, very dark. For me it often starts off in a dark place, but I can change things. I can see it all from here, no matter that it is dark it makes no difference to me. High up from my central vantage point on this bitter cold night my mind is clear as I float high over the city.

Just an ordinary city, a place like any other where people of all types have been coming and going over the years. I see prominent buildings steeped in history, the streets, the roads and pathways, trodden by generation after generation. Patches of light spring up from the suburban clutter, and I know that from within each of them glows a story. And as I look beyond I see the green of the countryside where times long past merge with the present; where people have lived, loved, and died. Wherever I go I see *further* than the dark of a bitter cold night – much further.

Peterborough, this city, just like any other, has a history formed by its people, their lives and experiences. These are people just like you and me, no matter how important or how insignificant things may seem, they have many stories to tell . . . and they don't always play out the way that we might expect them to.

Where am I?

My mind is distracted as I look south towards the bridge and over the river. I remember sitting there once with my grandson and telling him some of the many fascinations that had taken place locally, about which most people knew very little. For a moment I feel it all seems so long ago but then I realise time remains still with me now.

Suddenly, I'm standing on the top floor of a car park, and as I look eastwards across the city, I can see all the outlines of prominence. The large and noble illumination in front of me seems almost like a computer generated image against the deep Prussian blue sky with many other buildings making up the menagerie. I stare as the splendid Cathedral beckons me — as if it's trying to speak. I can feel its power.

The sharp sound of clear footsteps cuts through the cold night air as it is projected towards me. I momentarily freeze. I can hear the voices now — two voices! I look on, as still I float.

Through the slatted wooden doorway on the top floor of the car park I feel the shuffling footsteps of two people; a couple. As I peer, knowing that they can't see me, I make little effort to bother comprehending their low tones of jovial conversation. But I recognise them. I remember them as I start to drift away from the city centre.

My mind palace opens, and now I glance to the north east, beyond that most sacred and splendid building. I float higher into the night sky as I start to recall, and I head out of the city into the dark abyss. I can see a patch of light opening a mile or two beyond. Ah! The light is now that of an evening, yes . . . a late summer's evening . . . and this is the story that starts right here in that place, perhaps long ago, or maybe not so . . . but then, what matter is time?

❀ ❀ ❀ ❀ ❀

1. The Burial

Oxney Grange, Peterborough, 1433

The light was fading fast, he knew he had to be swift about his actions. Pressing his hand firmly against his side he shuffled through the shrubbery that surrounded the small copse. He repeated this gesture several times during the short journey, but there was really no need ... he hadn't dropped it. There wasn't time to stop and think this through, he just needed to get rid of it. No suitable occasion had presented itself and this thing was surely evil – he could feel it. So, with this limited window of opportunity, there seemed no better option than to bury it.

Scrambling through the undergrowth he saw the shovel he'd left behind earlier to aid him in his task was still there. This was a relief. It would only take a couple of minutes once he started to dig ... and he probably only *had* a couple of minutes.

"Richard!" A calm, but firm voice reverberated through the cool late summer evening air.

Damnation, I must be quick. Recognising the voice immediately, he continued to dig at a pace, knowing that he would be permanently disturbed from his task if he didn't respond in the next few seconds. The shallowest of trenches was all that was required before he could toss the malevolent object into the earth, and, almost with a continuous movement, use the remainder of the soil on his shovel to cover it over. It was while firmly implanting his light footwear onto the surface in an effort to quickly compress the soil, that his attention became instantly diverted. He'd certainly been disturbed, but not in the way he had expected.

Looking up towards where the noise was coming from – some thirty yards or so in front of him slightly to his right, he could see a figure moving swiftly in a direction that would soon bring it across his path. Nobody must see what he was doing, and there shouldn't be anyone roaming this way – not under *any* condition. Instinctively, he ducked, hoping to be obscured from the stranger's view by the foliage that lay between them. Straining to hold his breath he crouched and watched with a dappled view through the cover provided by the thick fresh leaves. What he then saw unfold in front of him seemed plainly wrong! There *was* a figure – a woman, and she was running. Her lips were parted, her eyes glazed with a fixed stare straight ahead, and her face was pale. But there was something else – her clothes, her garments – they were very strange. Staring, with his mouth hung open, time stood still. The shovel almost slipped through his fingers as in that split second came to him a strange sense of knowing what was to imminently follow. He could see that the woman, now in full view, was tall. He peered straight at her, but surely now his eyes were lying? How could this be? Instinctively he tightened his grip of the shovel, as if to reassure himself that what he could see was real. The features of the figure before him faded beneath the knees ... this woman walked without feet! Transfixed in that moment of time Richard watched as she then simply just disappeared from his view.

"Richard, Richard are you there?" The voice came once more, jolting him back to the reality of the moment. Quickly gathering himself, he rose to his feet, forced now to accept that his job was done.

"I'm here brother ... I'm coming," he panted. *John was so*

intense at times, couldn't he just wait?

Richard, somewhat in a state of shock, was certainly a little scared but also annoyed as he padded his way back along the pathway that led to the garden. His thick brown sleeves wiped the cold sweat from his brow as he went. Conflicting emotions scrambled his mind, he needed to think quickly.

"I just needed a stroll." He smiled at John as he delivered these words hoping it would be enough; he didn't really want to get drawn into explaining himself any more. John was a calm chap. He never looked to seek the challenge, or question the strange or unusual, he just got on with his relatively simple life. Tonight of all nights, this was blessing for Richard.

❈ ❈ ❈ ❈ ❈

The next morning he awoke earlier than usual before everyone else. The previous evening's events were at the forefront of his mind. Who was that figure he'd seen by the woods last night? Was she an apparition? Could he even believe in such things? He was confused, but it was something else that had been bothering him constantly over the last few weeks that had led to him not being able to sleep at all well. Right now, this preyed heavily on his mind. Something far more serious had happened recently over which he was having real trouble reconciling his logical thoughts with his conscience.

There had been a disagreement – a pretty serious one. It was not uncommon for any of them to fall out over various matters. Outsiders would perhaps be surprised, they didn't know or understand the intensity of the life style and the pressure of the boredom. However, this time it had all gone horribly wrong: They had left the building and headed into the village where they had all drunk heavily. When they returned very late, far the worse for wear due to the alcohol, the disagreement had escalated into a full-on fight and now, as a result ... someone was dead! Surely, they would end up with the same punishment as anybody else if they were caught? Their position would not protect them. The trouble was, nobody really seemed to care, nobody was checking up on them; that's why it had all got terribly out of hand.

Richard gazed out of his window across the vegetable garden and towards the woodland area beyond. This wasn't a bad place to be living, heaven knows it could be worse. In this day and age, some folk didn't even have two pennies to rub together. It was just three miles to the centre of the town, and although they say the land starts to get flat and boring as you head East, their position was quite secure, on a decent lie of land to the North east of the city. The problem now was that they were all living their lives right on the edge, they knew the wrong they had done and were just waiting to be found out. He wasn't just talking about himself and John either, Peter and the others felt the same way too – surely they did.

Richard felt the gape deep down in the pit of his stomach as he started to vividly recall the recent events. It had all happened so quickly, and, because they were all rather inebriated at the time, nobody could remember with complete clarity just what had taken place on that fateful evening. Dominic didn't deserve it, he knew that. What happened was just the very worst thing, but it wasn't just down to Peter; pure evil had taken hold of him. He hadn't meant it, he'd just lost it completely. It was of no use going over all of this now, the damage was done. He'd had to deal with death before, and now they all had to deal with it, but this time, they couldn't let it get out . . . it would have to be covered up.

Dominic wouldn't be missed because they were his closest companions. He had no one else, and his background was a little shady. Now, *they* would be looking for all of them, not just Peter, but John, himself, and the rest. They would all be found out, of course they would ... hunted down ... he felt sure of it. What on this earth could affect things to turn out any differently? Worst of all, the body had been buried in the grounds already – they'd even held a ceremony of sorts.

Drawing a deep breath he felt quite sick as he recalled the order of events, and, frankly, this was all just so wrong! How could the others *not* be feeling the same?

Later that day, having said very little to anyone, the fear within him grew intolerably stronger, and the nightmare started to become reality.

He could see Peter moving towards him at speed along the trackway that aligned the fields to the South west of the big old property. He was waving his arms frantically – a warning? Richard couldn't make out any audible sounds at first, then, as Peter's stride grew stronger and his urgency became obvious, he could hear that he was repeating just two words over and over:

"He's coming . . . he's coming!"

His throat became quickly dry as his heartbeat quickened, this was going to be awkward, he hadn't reckoned on this occurring so soon.

Peter used some more words once he was close enough to catch his breath, but they were wasted on Richard – his mind was already racing ahead. Peter ran inside to tell the others. As he turned to look into the distance, he could just make out the figures, slightly in advance of the horizon, where the field line merged with the vague grey images of the distant dwellings at the edge of the town. Now, to be out of the way before they came – this was what they had planned as a cover story: Dominic was sick and Richard had taken him away to a friend to be looked after, out in the village of Eye, only about a mile and a half to the North. If *both* of them were missing it would seem far more plausible than just saying: *'Oh, Dominic? He's gone off somewhere'* or *'Don't know where he is today, I'm sure he'll be back later.'*

They were *all* supposed to be there, they couldn't hide, there would be no let off. Now that it was apparent that *he* really was on his way, and with an entourage ... most probably to check up on them, the plan just had to work.

So, shortly after, Richard found himself back in that same woodland copse, not more than about sixty yards from the house – the same place he'd been scared out of his wits just that evening before. There hadn't been time to get further away, there would be the risk of him being seen by either *himself*, or certainly one of his close associates. Their cover would be blown if that was to happen. No, while Peter, John, and the rest explained away in an effort to cover up the evil deed, he would lie low. He scrambled through the same shrubbery, brushed with the same trees and trod the same ground, feeling as if fate had taken a hold ... as if this was where he was destined to be – where he might be found and where it might all end! At that moment he felt so low, so hopelessly and unwittingly involved in something so evil.

Why did Peter do it? Why had he ripped the necklace from Richard's own neck, and, in an uncontrollable drunken rage, used it on another? But perhaps more importantly, why had Richard ever bothered to claim it back?

Well, the answer to this lies in human nature, our instinctive desire to know – to want to own and claim, and our chemical drive to investigate. It is why wars start, and how world problems are solved. It's what makes us human. Richard was no different from the rest of us:

When Richard realised the neck-chain was missing, he'd panicked. So, when Peter told him about a woman he'd seen passing in the distance stooping to pick something up from near to the very spot where the evil act had taken place, he'd dashed, fleet of foot across country to the woman's known residence – a cottage at the edge of the village where she lived with her father. As he cautiously approached the front of the building passing by the small window, he saw her sitting. He tapped the window to get her attention not realising she was asleep, he certainly hadn't meant to startle her. He pointed past the window towards the door as an indication to her to let him in. She did so. Almost as soon as he began to explain his predicament, she'd gone quietly to a drawer in a nearby desk to retrieve the neck-chain which she had found and placed there for safe keeping. She had returned it gracefully. Right now he wondered why he'd ever bothered to reclaim it, there seemed to be little point.

What was it that was so important about this artefact ... this necklace of Richard's? Well, he had worn it for as long as he could remember, even as a boy this necklace was with him. It belonged to his mother whom he didn't remember as she had died when he was very small. The others generally wore a large cross hung from a simple cord, but Richard's necklace was different; it was far more ornate than most neck-pieces. It boasted beads that had been beautifully crafted from pewter and sandal wood, and it was finished with a simple solemn cross of bronze. The others knew it held some significance of great importance to Richard but nobody knew quite what.

Maybe that is why in that terrible moment it was *chosen?* After all, there had been other things at hand! Perhaps this was why at that moment in time Richard felt it was inextricably part of him and therefore was driven to retrieve it.

As he stood on the very spot where he had buried the object of evil cause some eighteen hours earlier, he could almost feel its negative vibe. Was its evil curse now upon *him?*

This was by no means the end for Richard, not that day, that week, or even that month, and certainly not in that place.

❁ ❁ ❁ ❁ ❁

2. Surprise in the Post

Peterborough, April, 2014

Nasra Chowdhury rolled over on to her back as the piercing sound of the alarm clock rang through her head. She rubbed her eyes and hauled herself clear of the duvet. Grabbing her gown from the back of the door she shuffled through to the kitchen of her small single-bedroom flat. The early April sun beamed through the chink in the blinds causing her to squint as she lifted the kettle from its base and reached for the tap.

Nasra wasn't a morning person: she much preferred to do the later shifts, but the fact is in this industry you have to take what comes. Her job as a health and social care worker was rewarding at times but always demanding and today was likely to be just that. Her flat, in the suburb of Hampton, to the South of the city was a lucky catch for a single girl on her wage. If it wasn't for her friend Judy personally knowing the landlord and being quick to recommend her, she might never have got in when she did. The steep steps that lead up from the road are annoying, and the damn door always sticks, but it's not a bad place to live by any means – and the office is quite nearby, although her job takes her all over the city.

Having made herself a coffee, she sat at the table scrolling her smart phone with one hand while running the other through the strands of her jet black hair. *Mrs. Robertson first,* she thought to herself. *She'll be wanting me to feed her cat again no doubt.* (Last week her client had seemed pre-occupied with this and showed little interested in her own needs.) Her eyes rolled up towards the clock as it ticked through 7:00am. She sipped her coffee, clasping the mug. *Better hit the shower.*

Minutes later, Nasra emerged from the shower wrapped in white. Moving swiftly across towards the bedroom, she let out a squeal as her foot jarred on something in the carpet. The living area was full of clutter and things often got out of place. There were books in piles of twos and threes on arm rests, the coffee table, and down by the side of chairs. There wasn't a bookshelf in spite of Nasra being a voracious reader of all sorts of material. To the far side of the room was a table, but there weren't any chairs. She used the table partly as a place to stash various bits and pieces but also for something else; currently laid out in the corner was the start of a jigsaw puzzle taking shape. The unlaid pieces were piled up on the edge of the table, and it was one of these stray pieces that had fallen and caught in the pile of the carpet that she had just trodden on. Rubbing the sole of her foot she took her place at the dressing table and started to apply her make up.

A busy day lay ahead of her, life had been one continuous roller-coaster routine of work, sleep, repeat, since Christmas, and sometimes, on days like this it got to her. She continued to dress, and it was as she straightened the stiff white collar of her blouse with one hand and brushed her beige jacket with the other, there came the familiar shuffling sound of post dropping through the letterbox. She took one final look at herself in the mirror, throwing it a smug smile before darting across the hallway to pick up the small heap of envelopes that had landed on her mat. Thumbing through, she ignored a couple of circulars and another brown envelope. *Obviously a service bill,* she thought. Then she came to a package with a handwritten address on the front. Did she recognise the handwriting? For a split second she thought so, but didn't dwell on it. Inside was a letter. She opened it . . . more of a note really. Nasra's eyes widened as she took in the words as they were meant to sound – a kind and simple testimony. This was from an old lady she had cared for a while back. Slowly, as she read through the letter, the smiling face of that elderly woman imprinted itself on her mind, helping her recall the events of that day a few months ago for which now this lady seemed to be so grateful.

Her work mainly involved visiting individuals who needed support. It was emotionally tiring but rewarding and the days could be very varied. Sometimes it involved taking on-site sleep-overs, such was the nature of the necessary level of care required. It was one of these lengthy sessions to which she had been assigned on this particular day about which the old lady was thanking her for in her note:

She'd arrived in Fletton at the home of Eileen O'Darcy at 6.30 that evening very tired and stressed. As usual Eileen asked if she could make her a cup of tea . . . and to have one for herself too of course. This was a fairly common pattern, usually the first thirty minutes or so were spent chatting cosily – all part of the job. She hadn't been particularly looking forward to it on this occasion and she was secretly hoping that perhaps Eileen would be very tired, then she could at least relax a little. That night, however, was to take on a different turn of significance.

"Ooh! Pass me that brew could you," Eileen hitched herself up to a sitting position in the bed. "Ah, that's better."

Nasra asked how the week had gone and how she had been keeping.

"Not too bad my dear, thank you. Nice and peaceful, not like last Saturday."

"Last Saturday?" Nasra questioned.

"Well the noise ya' see ... coming from round the corner. He's always having parties and people round. No good ever comes of 'em ya' know."

"It's what people do these days I'm afraid. If it gets too bad we'll have to report it," Nasra replied.

Eileen grabbed her arm.

"Don't get involved." She said, staring Nasra hard in the eyes "Now, there's something more important I need you to do for me," she said.

"Oh!" Nasra remarked. This was a change of mood. Eileen looked across the room, a watery film now covered her eyes.

"Means a lot to me ya' see. Silly me, I should never have dropped it."

Her voice cracked slightly.

"What have you dropped?"

"I was only bending down to pick up a sweetie paper ... over there by the sideboard." Eileen waved an arm, pointing vaguely. Nasra followed the direction of her arm movements but it gave her very little information. "It just slipped off, and as luck would have it, went through the crack . . . all in one go!"

"Through the crack? What ... in the floorboards?" Nasra was getting the picture: The silly old bird had somehow lost some prized piece of adornment by letting it fall through the crack in the floorboards, and now she wanted her to try and retrieve it. This was frustrating, but she knew what was coming next.

"Please can you try and get it for me? It's very valuable and it means so much to me."

Hard though this might be, Nasra couldn't disappoint, it was part of her job.

She got herself over to the corner of the room where the red rosewood sideboard stood. Now, she could see that the floorboards had actually moved, and the wood had split and been chipped away slightly where a natural knot had once been. *This must be where it has fallen through.*

Poking a finger in the hole quickly established that it was not quite big enough. Taking her mobile phone she shone the torchlight through the crack. *Now what was this?* A sharply reflected glisten greeted her. If she could just work gently away at the slightly dry, rotted wood ... and make the hole a little larger ... *Eyebrow tweezers* she thought. She got up and crossed the room to where her bag was, then produced the required tool. Virtually lying across the floor, with one hand she shone the light from her mobile phone, as her other hand carefully guided the small metal pincers to their task. After just a few seconds she was able to extract the prized piece.

As she pulled the bracelet gently free from its resting place something quite weird happened. A strong feeling of powerful attachment forced a desire within her to not let go. The more she thought it the more it seemed to amplify within her. She found herself caressing each of the plain, flat stone-like imbedded gems. It was as if this was meant to be – her, holding this bracelet right at that moment. She looked briefly across at Eileen who sat beaming across from the bed. Then, as she staggered back across the room forcing herself to hand the piece of adornment triumphantly back to its rightful owner, it became a very special moment: *This is like the captain of some great sport team winning back the trophy that has long since been in alien hands, and then taking it home,* she thought.

Eileen was ecstatic as Nasra remembered. She began telling the whole history of the bracelet, and how her dear Edward had given it to her as a 10th anniversary present back in the nineteen sixties. How it had been with her through good times and bad and how she was sure it had brought her good luck on more than one occasion. She went on to tell Nasra about one of the worst things that ever happened to her and how the bracelet had *saved* her and Edward:

They were apparently mugged on the way home from a night out many years ago. Edward was roughed up a bit and the gang threatened Eileen and tried to take the bracelet from her. When it became clear that a terrified Eileen was having some difficulty in handing it over, each gang member tried in turn, but couldn't prize it from her wrist;

"It were never gonna leave me ya' see," Eileen was proud of this moment on reflection, having forgotten her fear at the time as she told this story. "Attached itself good and proper it did .. and that's when they came .."

"They?" Nasra was curious as to how this tale was to end.

"People – from the other side of the street. Those ruffians weren't concentrating ... took too long trying to get the bracelet ... got outnumbered and ran off ya' see."

Eileen firmly believed that on at least this one occasion the bracelet had been integral to their safekeeping.

So, what had Eileen said to Nasra in the letter that had arrived that morning?

Well, she'd actually *given* her the bracelet. She wanted her to have it, she said it would bring her good luck and that she deserved it. It was up to her how she used it.

For a moment Nasra just stared at the bubble-wrapped bulge in the envelope while she recalled the emotions of the day she retrieved it. Then, she opened the package and once again held the bracelet of Eileen's in her hands. A strange sensation ran through her, like a warm glow that started at her finger-tips and spread all over. It just felt good. She clasped the bracelet tightly in her hand for a moment, but then, as her gaze veered towards the wall clock she was reminded of the urgent need to leave for work. She placed the bracelet on the side as she grabbed her jacket.

3. Judy and Nasra

It was early the next evening and Nasra was running late, as usual. She reached up to slot the key in the lock of her flat door as she struggled with her bags of shopping. Giving the door a persuasive kick and turning with her back towards it, clasping the heaviest bag to her stomach, she made her way inside her flat.

Dumping the shopping down on the kitchen table, she took a deep breath. *Don't really want to go out tonight, much rather have a quiet evening in front of the TV. Sorry Judy,* she thought to herself, kicking off her shoes and moving through to the living room. She couldn't get herself past the table in the corner set against the wall; the distraction always got her. The box said fifteen hundred pieces, but it seemed more like fifteen thousand! Jigsaws were big in Nasra's life right now, and she loved completing them. After the time a couple of years back when a bout of hepatitis had dumped her in hospital, and her mum had brought her one to do, she had become quite an addict. Last summer her friend returned from holiday with a boxed set; *Cornish Villages,* all large format and well over a thousand pieces. She had worked her way through that in just a week or so. Lately, there had always been a puzzle laid out somewhere in the flat that she could keep going back to. The particular puzzle she had on the go presently was just called *Peterborough.* It had images from the past and present in the four corners with the Cathedral set in the middle.

She sifted through a pile of grey-coloured pieces that she

had collected the night before and placed to the side. She squinted, cocking her head towards the box lid. *These were all surely part of the wall at the front of the picture.* She pushed aside the flow of her long jet-black hair as she tried to decide which piece should go where.

There wasn't time now, she should really move on. After a minute or two, tired and frustrated, she stretched her arms above her head and let out a yawn. As she did so the bracelet on her right wrist slipped down her forearm. It was a bit too big for her but that didn't matter. She just decided that morning that she should wear it.

Touching the bracelet with her other hand she immediately felt something powerful . . . this had happened earlier as well when during a social care meeting she had nearly looked silly because she couldn't remember a statistic she should have known. Nervously she had clasped her hands together, and when she was reminded of the surprise received in the post that she was now wearing, the figures suddenly came to her mind.

As she thought this through the prospect of going out tonight now wasn't so daunting, Mrs. Cooper, who she had helped earlier in the day as part of her job didn't seem so grumpy after all, and, as she stared across at the teal wall of her living room, it was now a much more appealing colour to the eye. Nasra had never been one to allow herself to get a fixation with things, but this was different, she was getting some real positive vibe from it. Looking back down at the puzzle her lips slowly broke into a curl and she laughed to herself out loud. *'That's it! That's where it fits. Why couldn't I see that before?'* Her fingers pressed the piece firmly into place.

❖ ❖ ❖ ❖ ❖

About an hour later a small woman with light brown hair sat alone on a seat in the Queensgate shopping centre. It was Thursday and very busy. She glanced at her watch then scanned the walkway but there was no sign of her friend yet. To her left were the escalators that led to the second floor; in front of her and to her right were the myriad of shops open for late night shopping.

Directly in front was a children's clothes shop and the sign at the front immediately caught her attention. There was a sale – *'Babywear, and age 5 and below'*. There was no sign of Nasra yet so she got up to go and have a closer look. She and her husband Neil had been together a few years now and she knew Neil would love to start a family too. A wry smile spread across her face as this thought sank in.

Come on Nasra, she thought, looking left and right along the indoor precincts. Neil will be done before we've started shopping at this rate.

Neil was bowling with his work mates; somebody was leaving and this was what they had chosen to do for their leaving party. The bowling alley was only about six or seven minutes walk from the shopping centre and the plan was that they would walk and meet the guys after they had finished their shopping. Judy Pressland hoped that this would do her other half some good: he had been a little stressed in recent months, but at last, just lately things with him were settling down a bit. This was the first time he had been out with his mates for a while and Judy was pleased that he was socialising again. Her train of thought was interrupted by the approaching sound, the clack of high heels on a hard floor, accompanied by a familiar voice calling her name.

The two friends hugged and exchanged pleasantries before

then getting down to the important decision-making process of where they should head first. They walked and they talked and they looked in shop after shop, parting with their money as they saw fit, but if the truth be known, both of them were really most interested in the last stop – the Coffee shop. Judy was tired and would have happily missed this arrangement but she didn't want to let her friend down, and besides, there had been no chance to catch up for a week or two. As they browsed all their regular haunts, it became evident to Judy that her friend was not her usual bubbly self, she seemed preoccupied with something.

"So, are you going to tell me what's up?" Judy asked.

Nasra's mouth dropped and she gave her friend a vacant stare.

"Come on, there is something ... I've known you too long."

So, Nasra told her friend about what had happened yesterday morning. Judy listened passively, hearing the words but only partially processing them. Judy's concentration was poor, she kept changing the subject back to the jacket she had just bought, and did Nasra think it was the right colour for her, or should she wear something with a bit more blue now summer was approaching? But as Nasra kept steering the conversation back to the subject, Judy found herself becoming drawn in.

"I was so shocked you see, I would just never have expected to receive anything like it as a gift ... from anyone."

Nasra told her friend the story of the kind old lady and how she had passed on the bracelet she valued so much to her.

"I mean why did she give it to me? It meant so much to *her*.

Why didn't she just reward me some other way if she felt so grateful?"

It wasn't that Nasra was not one hundred percent grateful to be given the piece, it was actually that she felt a little guilty, a little unworthy perhaps to be wearing it. She felt she had to explain this to Judy.

"Well, could be that she just thinks it suits you better. I mean, if she really believes it has the power to help, what good is it to her now? She's an old lady – probably thinks any 'good luck' it might bring would be wasted on herself."

Nasra hadn't thought of it quite like that.

The two of them sat for a moment without speaking. Nasra wondered if she should ask:

"How are things ... I mean with you and Neil?" She was greeted with a steel-eyed stare. "I mean, you were worried about him last time we spoke."

"He's ok, just gets a bit stressed about things now and then." Judy said, gazing past her friend, not wanting to make eye contact.

"So what does he get stressed about? You are alright ... you two?"

Judy smiled.

"Yeah, we are good. I just worry about what he's up to sometimes ... you know ... when he goes out and comes back late. Sometimes I worry because he never tells me."

Nasra could read the concern on her friend's face.

"You don't think he's taking anything?" (She had meant this to sound more like a statement.) Judy screwed up her face, no way was he on anything ... but could she be sure? Whatever, she wasn't going to go down this road with her friend:

"No. Neil doesn't take stuff, but he does get involved ... " Judy's voice buckled and she couldn't finish her sentence.

"He gets involved with some people who might and you wish he wouldn't?" Nasra finished it for her.

"I guess so." Judy glanced at her watch, she didn't want to say any more.

"We had better be making our way over to the bowling arcade. They will be finished in about twenty minutes." The two women rose to their feet, Judy much the more tired.

She was flustered and was eager to keep the rendezvous on time so they could all get home and fix something to eat before the evening was gone. She directed her friend to a short cut through the Cathedral precincts which would be their quickest route to get to the agreed meeting place on time.

Wobbling slightly with the laden carrier bags that made her somehow feel twice her true weight, she wished her friend would slow down. Nasra was moving a little too quickly for her.

"What time did you say to Neil?" she said looking back over her shoulder.

"7.30 at the bowling alley car park," panted Judy.

"We've got five minutes then."

"Wait up" she called. "I can't go as fast as you."

Suddenly, the bag parted company with its contents and slipped from Judy's grasp as she looked across towards the Cathedral.

Nasra stopped, realising that she had been slightly thoughtless in her efforts to plunge on ahead and that it was too much for Judy to keep up. As she back-tracked the ten metres to help her friend she followed Judy's gaze; Judy had stopped still and was looking to a spot in the shadows at the side of the great building about fifty metres away.

"What's he doing here ... ?" Judy's voice tailed off dreamily. Nasra scrutinised a figure wearing an odd-looking 'hoodie' of sorts, pacing hurriedly up and down. She knew what her friend was thinking and wanted to check it out for herself.

"Neil?" Judy was gobsmacked.

"No, no, that's not Neil." Her friend corrected her somewhat churlishly, wondering how she had mistaken some other similar-looking guy for her own husband. It was a bit strange, the light wasn't that bad! "Come on, let's get this lot picked up, it's nearly 7.30." Nasra bent to help pick up the spilt goods.

4. The Stranger in the Precinct

Peterborough Abbey, August 1433

Time passed and it appeared that they had got away with it. At least, this is how Richard saw it, but there was a high price to pay, and an uncomfortable load to bear. It preyed heavily on his mind every single day, and, as if that wasn't enough, over the next few weeks there were to be constant reminders.

Richard had journeyed back some three miles to the centre of the city. After all this was where he should be spending his time, not out in the countryside away from it all. John had come with him, but Peter; he'd stayed out in the country. It was his decision and he felt that suspicion could be alleviated if he stayed. It would also give him some time to work things out properly. Who knows what the future holds? They prayed daily, their faith was now tested to the full. Richard felt strongly that they all had a duty to try and put right some of the wrong wherever they could.

So Richard spent his days working, thinking, praying and hoping with all the faith bestowed upon him that he could get on and lead his life the way God had intended. The trouble was, he kept seeing her – the girl he'd seen in the woods weeks before. While walking through the gardens to the East of the City's most sacred building, he glimpsed her, bustling along the edge of the grounds. Then, on another occasion strolling towards the old vegetable gardens and under a main archway, there she was again. This time she appeared dressed in tight fitting clothing that showed her outline form in a most peculiar way as she appeared to lope from side to side, evidentially weighed down by the baggages she carried in either hand. Each time Richard saw this vision she would disappear into thin air after just a few seconds.

One morning in late June, a very strange thing happened. The sun was warm this day, uncomfortably so. Mopping his brow, he fancied taking the short cut across the grass back to his living quarters. But then, almost immediately he stopped, quite startled. This was most peculiar, surely those were voices . . . and several voices at that. Looking around he could see no one. He hadn't felt at all well lately and he did now start to wonder if he might be going mad! But then, suddenly, just as he had ascertained for himself that the green area in front of him, the shrubbery and the nearby trees were completely uninhabited by anyone, into view came a man. It was unusual to see anyone there in the central gardens at that time and so both men would have been embarrassed if they tried to avoid the mandatory pleasantries of acknowledgement. Richard nodded, smiling as they approached each other. The man had simply *appeared* in front of him. This man was also dressed strangely, just like the apparition of the woman he had so often seen. His legs were covered with a tight-fitting garment and Richard could see his eyes were distant, not wanting to meet his own. Richard felt he had to speak:

"Are you well sir? Can I be of any help to you?"

The stranger stood still abruptly, his hand went to a pocket, as if he was about to produce something. He raised his eyes and looked at Richard, his mouth open ready to speak. Richard felt a strange sensation; he became suddenly full of fear; a feeling of instant regret at the mere asking of the question as if it was the trigger for something quite momentous to take place, and yet outwardly, this man posed no threat to him. But what was he thinking? This was ridiculous, after all it was he himself who offered to help!

"Yes, I reckon you can help," replied the stranger after taking a second or two to gather his thoughts. "Brother, I have something for you."

Richard looked straight at him, his eyes slightly widened. The stare was one of utter disbelief as he felt he knew what was coming next. Those words rang through his head like the Angelus bell that called him daily to fulfil a duty he could never deny. They became imprinted on his mind at that very moment and signified the start of his whole world being about to change.

❄ ❄ ❄ ❄ ❄

It all happened very quickly in the end, and we will never know exactly whether things might have been any different for Richard if that fateful night months earlier had never taken place. I suspect not. Our lives follow a course that is mapped out for us: we journey down life's path hoping to discover a new destination but nearly always in history people have found themselves standing firm, leading the lives they were born to lead.

And so it was for Richard. He had been sent with the others out to the Grange as a punishment. A terrible act then followed; murder, manslaughter, (call it what you will), had been committed with something that belonged to him. It felt to Richard as if it was *he* who had been caught red-handed with the murder weapon. Ever since that day he'd met the stranger who saw him as a brother, seemingly intent on returning it to him, fear and insecurity had become harboured all around him.

The country didn't have a clear leader at this time, unrest and insecurity amongst society was prevalent. What else could be expected when a boy, nothing more than a mere child had taken the throne of England? The Abbot, John Deeping was not someone Richard could confide in, and so as the next few weeks of his simple monastic life passed, all that fear, guilt and insecurity bred in Richard an illness from which he was never to recover.

By the late summer of 1433 Brother Richard had developed a high fever. His close friends, brothers John and now Peter too were at his side that afternoon as he attempted to recount to them what seemed like some sort of dream he'd had in which he was convinced that he'd been given, and now had in his possession an 'evil artefact'. It must be got rid of before it was too late! Accepting that this was all delirium brought on by the fever, Peter and John nevertheless went to look for it above the fireplace as Richard had instructed . . . but of course . . . there was nothing there!

Later, on that evening of 27th August 1433, Richard's journey of anguish finally ended as his life became the past.

5. Three Friends

Peterborough, April 2014

The next evening the three were together. Judy had told her friend how they had got into the habit of going out once a month to a pub on Lincoln Road and if Nasra could join them, it would make a nice evening and the three of them could catch up properly. Nasra had been Judy's friend since childhood, but Neil had got to know her quite well too over recent years.

"Anyway, you haven't told me about your new job yet." Nasra was addressing Neil.

"Oh, it's kind of okay really. Different from what I was doing before with the agency though, and definitely better."

Neil had recently got a job with a small engineering firm in Eastfield, on the oldest industrial estate in a city that now boasts a tapestry of them.

"What do you do?" She asked, genuinely interested.

"Welding mainly ... and loads of lifting." Neil's eyes shaped to a squint and his head nodded slightly as he delivered these words, pulling that face guys pull when they want you to know 'it's hard work but we are tough enough to take it.'

"We make frames, all sorts of metal frames ... for display stands. Metal crate main structures ... loads of different stuff really."

"That sounds cool, I'm glad it's going well." Nasra reached for her drink. It was good to see that Neil was happy and settled.

Judy huddled up to her partner and clenched his hand firmly.

"We're good," she said. "You're settled in that job now aren't you? And life's been really good to us the last few months, hasn't it?" She wasn't expecting answers, she just looked up at Neil, seeking approval for this last comment. He smiled back at her.

"Now you've got your act together," she continued, grinning, and delivering a friendly prod to his arm. "Now that you're not '*spooked out*' all the time."

"Spooked out?" Nasra wanted to know more. Neil smiled at them both.

"Go on ... tell her about that night." Neil grinned at his wife, slightly surprised at the invitation, but he didn't need much cajoling. It was a story he had enjoyed telling a few times now.

"Well, I was on late shift with my mate Alfie, and he told me about the ghost that's been seen on the second floor at our place. Apparently it's someone who used to work there but died in an accident one night on his way home. The story goes that the last thing he did was turn off the machinery before clocking out. He was a very conscientious person, and he comes back – to check up on things when people work late."

"Hmm, interesting ... so where do you fit in?" Nasra was curious.

"Go on ..." Judy encouraged him to continue.

"Well, people say I'm like ... well, a bit sort of ... I've got second sight." He blurted out his words.

"How do you mean?" This was becoming amusing; what did he mean by *second-sight?* Where was he going with this? Was he really saying that he had some kind of special ability?

"Well, I don't know really, I think it's because of the fact that this ghost always seemed to appear when I was on the late shift ... but I never saw it!"

"You never saw it?"

"Nah, always seemed to be someone else."

Now it was becoming hard for Nasra not to laugh.

"And you are supposed to be the one with the second sight?" She couldn't help but grin.

"Go on ... tell her the rest." His partner encouraged him with a nudge in the ribs.

"Well, I think it's really because of the tests."

"The tests?" Nasra put her hand to her face to cover her creeping smile, feeling an uncontrollable urge to giggle.

"Well, my mates took the mickey a bit and started asking me other things about ghosts, and it seems that I came up trumps with some of the answers."

Managing to control herself, Nasra found herself now quite hooked by the angle of quirkiness the conversation was taking.

"Meaning exactly?"

"Well, we all got talking about ghost stories, and I suppose we were trying to impress each other – as you do. One day I just came out with this story about something that apparently happened round about here years ago ... involving some old fuddy-duddy!"

His eyes darted from Nasra to Judy. Neil paused.

"And?"

"Well that's just it you see. I can't even remember the details I came up with, but my mate turned up the next day – said he'd researched it all on the internet and everything I'd said to him was exactly as it was supposed to have happened all those years ago. So you see, they think I've got it." Neil tapped his forehead. "I think it's all a bit silly myself."

This was all very interesting but the most likely explanation was a combination of the luck of predictability and exaggeration. People always want to believe a good spooky story, it adds to the mystery. Nasra was a bright woman and could see how this worked. She didn't want to be disrespectful to her friends. Yes, she could challenge him, but that surely would burst his bubble and he didn't need that right now. And Judy? Well, she was gazing proudly at her other half as if he'd just accomplished something really important by telling this story. There was more to this; it was something in the way that Neil had just given that account; he used the past tense an awful lot considering this was apparently still happening at the place he went to work every day. She chose her words carefully:

"You said this is what *was* happening; these things – you

talk about them all in the past tense?"

Judy again answered for Neil:

"They don't happen any more. This all stopped a few weeks ago didn't it?" she looked at Neil once more as if for a prompt. Nothing came, he just smiled sheepishly at both women, so Judy continued:

"He got quite worked up about it at the time, didn't you? He was coming home and telling me all about who'd said what to him and what he'd said back. At the time it seemed quite funny. Then, it all stopped quite suddenly, and I noticed a difference. You weren't so worked up and angry about things. You seemed calmer." She smiled up at Neil, who sat passively in silence.

This had been interesting to hear but Nasra suddenly now felt keen to change the subject.

"Well, as long as you're happy now, what the hell ... ghosts hey!"

The three of them spent another hour or so in *The Paul Pry*: the restaurant and public house situated on Lincoln Road in the Walton area north of Peterborough City centre just a couple of miles from where Neil and Judy lived in North Bretton. They talked about the past, and the things they had got up to as teenagers a decade or more ago. They recalled places they had visited, the good times they'd had, and how the passing of years had changed them, as the completion of a third decade loomed closer for all three of them. It was when they were talking about these significant changes that Nasra remembered something else ... and she just had to ask:

"What happened to all the bling? You used to be pretty hot

with wearing the stuff as I remember . . . the old *Medallion man* image?" Neil had gone through a phase where he liked to wear chains, necklaces, bracelets – the lot. At one time, as Nasra remembered, he had looked a little ridiculous. Nasra grinned at Neil, rocking slightly from side to side, wondering how Neil would answer her.

"Oh, that all stopped." Judy was quite emphatic as she chipped in once again. "He used to wear all sorts of stuff including that silly old thing." Neil's lips parted slightly and his eyes narrowed as he threw her a look of slight discomfort. He knew she was about to delve deeper into their past in order to explain this last remark.

What was Judy about to tell them? Neil was clearly a little apprehensive about where this one was going. Nasra was ready to listen.

6. One Summer's Evening

Judy Pressland is a quiet-natured person and rarely speaks up in company. Back in school she would never put her hand up to answer a question unless she absolutely had to. But as the three of them sat in the city pub that evening she was able to recount to her friend and husband in great detail a story that took place over a decade earlier, shortly after she and Neil had first met.

❈ ❈ ❈ ❈ ❈

August 29th 2003:

It was a late summer's evening as Judy cautiously made her way down Eyebury Road. The village of Eye to the north of Peterborough was where her home was. It is an old village unspoiled by the modern development that has taken place in other areas of the city. Then, as now, you can be walking in countryside within five minutes of wherever in the village you live. The Eyebury Road heads south and leads out to the edge of the flat fenland that runs between Peterborough and Whittlesey.

On this occasion she was on her way to investigate; there was something she had to see for herself. She made her way out of the village, striding, with a deliberate purpose about her actions. People had told her, so surely it *was* all going to turn out to be true? After all, rumours don't usually propagate without some substance, but she had to be sure; if the building really had burned down then she needed to see it for herself ...

tonight.

They hadn't meant any harm, none of them really wanted to cause any trouble but it looked as if somehow their plan had gone awry. A derelict house, a creepy dare, that's all was, but if *he* was going along then she wanted to be there too. She'd had a crush on him for a few weeks now, but no real relationship was forming. He was just going through that showing off phase where everything he did seemed to be designed to impress. Judy wasn't always sure how deliberate it was, but right now, this side of his nature left her feeling a little uncomfortable.

As she passed the last house on the edge of the village, the chill of the late summer breeze hit her. In front sprawled flat desolate farmland offering a long straight walk ahead to the next landmark, a solitary building some distance beyond. From there she would still have a bit of a trek to the place she had been two nights previously, the place that somehow got burned down – but it had *not* happened while she had been there.

Ten minutes later she was near enough for her worst fears to be confirmed. Clearly, there was now just a burned out wreckage where a large noble old property had until so recently stood. Judy stopped dead in her tracks, gazing, almost in disbelief at what she could see in front of her. Her breath became short as her heart felt suddenly heavy as if it had just physically dropped within her. Her mind started to relive the moments she had experienced the other night:

Four of them had gone there for a laugh – a dare. They were planning to stay there – not for the night or anything so dramatic, but probably until quite late. Mum and Dad would be okay with this, just as long as she got herself in by 10:30 pm. Judy did more or less what she liked in terms of stopping out with her mates; she never caused any trouble for her parents and they never asked any questions.

The small gang had ambled raucously along the same route to get to the building that she had just taken. It was quite early in the evening – still daylight. *He* was in a bit of a wild mood to say the least. He kept picking things up and throwing them and making silly fighting gestures with Rick, one of the other guys in the gang. And, at one point he picked up some old cap that was left at the side of the road and insisted on wearing it for the rest of the evening. This was all done mainly to impress her. She knew that.

When they got to the old place, they made their way inside through a half-broken window. There were lots of windows. The building was a tall two floors and had been derelict for some time. There was a lot of whispering and giggling as they each scanned the area before clambering inside, satisfying themselves that no one was around. It wasn't long before they were going through the motions: playing silly games, hiding and spooking each other ... you know the sort of stuff. This went on for some time and Judy started to get a bit fed up of it all. Events took a negative turn when *He* and Rick announced they were going to stay there for the night. The other guy with them that evening was some moron called Jake (probably Rick's buddy Judy reckoned). They started arguing about something, and so then, Jake stormed off!

Now Judy was left with a dilemma; she wanted to spend some time with him but this wasn't part of the plan. No way was she *actually* going to spend the night there, not under *any* condition. What was she to do? She basically had no choice other than to leave them to it and head off home. This had rather annoyed her to say the least. The two guys made some feeble effort to encourage her to stay but it wasn't long before she found herself walking alone, away from the building, and very quickly she started to feel just a tiny bit scared!

Now, as the light was fading fast she knew she had to be swift about her actions. She glanced back over her shoulder towards the old house. Its dark silhouette, startlingly dynamic against the deep blue sky backdrop, and broken only by the occasional streak of an evening cloud desperately trying to emit the last remnants of daylight through its fast closing cracks. *Ten minutes* she calculated, if she ran. Leaving the old house from the rear, (that's where they were at the time of the final friction-filled conversation), she would now have to scramble across the field and pass by the edge of the trees in order to get herself back on to the road. She started to run, and her heart was soon pounding, but nothing was going to stop her, not even the shuffling sound she imagined she could hear coming from the trees a few yards over to her left.

As Judy recalled these events of a few nights earlier with mixed emotions and a notable amount of unease, she decided now that she was close, she must force herself to take the thorough look over the old building that she'd always planned on having. *No point in coming all this way otherwise* she told herself. She resumed her stride, her eyes fixed glaringly on the deformed structure that stood in front of her. Pungent air containing the strong aroma associated with where a fire had recently been filled her lungs. It was then that she was suddenly stopped in her tracks. Her foot had trodden on something: Bending down, she scrutinised the object beneath her feet. This was that necklace thing *he'd* found, it must be. She allowed its chain to slip through her fingers. He must have dropped it the other night after she had left. She stopped still for a moment, remembering how he'd been picking things up, chucking them about, and trying on dirty headwear that he'd found on the ground just for a laugh. And this? Surely it was that thing he'd found that caused so much excitement. He reckoned it was some ancient relic – said it would bring him luck and he insisted on wearing it, so round his neck it went. She hadn't seen him since. She carefully folded it and placed it in her coat pocket. It was highly likely that the gang had needed to make a quick getaway. Yes, that was it ... he probably started the fire for a laugh or something then ran off. She could just picture it. *He must have dropped it, he'll be made up when I give it back to him.*

This could be a landmark point in their relationship, maybe he'd actually be grateful? Maybe he'd start to show some interest in her? *Maybe* he'd grow up a bit and actually start to think about the effect his actions were having on others?

Again, Judy started to feel a mix of emotions, but this time it was those of relief and happiness. She was not to be disappointed.

❄ ❄ ❄ ❄ ❄

"So, once I gave it back to him, that was it. We made up and we started going out. You've never done anything stupid like that since have you ..." Judy clasped Neil's arm and giggled as she delivered this remark.

Nasra had listened to every word; she was impressed with this story;

"I never knew. You haven't told me any of this before."

"Well, suppose not. It's not really something we go back over very often."

Neil clasped his hands together then parted them and rubbed his knees – clearly still a little embarrassed about the whole incident and his behaviour at the time, even though it had taken place more than ten years earlier.

Nasra and Neil both reached for their drinks at the same moment. There was a slightly awkward pause while Nasra sipped her Gin and tonic and Neil swigged his beer.

"But you still haven't told me about all that jewellery stuff — why you stopped wearing it? And that old relic, what was it?"

"Dunno." Neil replied dismissively. He looked at his partner before continuing "All I know is when I finally stopped, things sort of – well ... changed. So I guessed it was best if I just stopped wearing the jewellery altogether."

"It was when you stopped wearing that old necklace thing," chirped Judy. "that's when it got better, definitely."

"What do you mean?" Nasra was now more than curious.

"Well," began Judy, her eyes glancing to and fro' between her friend and partner, as if hoping for their anticipated approval of what she was about to say. "It was evil – that thing, don't you see? Remember when that bloke told us how things from the past can bring bad luck if they are cursed?" There was some animation in Judy's voice and a furrow appeared across Neil's brow as he placed his glass on the table and leaned back.

"That was on television, last year – some history documentary about when people used to believe all that stuff!"

"Yeah, well, maybe it was, but all the same, I say it brought us nothing but bad luck."

What Judy was saying was clearly important. She had retold the story with passion in her voice, and now, she believed that at least some of the events in their lives had been affected by the find all those years ago. She sat with her head held low, what was coming next?

"We had a rough time from when we first got together." Judy looked up at Neil who didn't respond. "I lost the baby." Judy lowered her head again and paused. Neil reached across and put his arm around her; she continued. "Then, we got flooded out – only house in Peterborough that did that year, remember? Nothing seemed to go right for us, it was one thing after another. You lost your job – twice!" She turned to her husband before continuing to tell Nasra the rest. Neil smiled blankly but said nothing. "We had no money, and I started to think, what had we done to deserve all this? Then, one day Neil said, you know what, this is all hogwash. He was fed up with people looking at him with all his jewellery: bracelets, necklaces and rings, etc., so he just stopped wearing them."

"I still wore that old necklace though, at least – it was the last thing to go."

Neil's expression rather reminded Nasra of a rabbit caught in car headlights.

"Yes, but don't you see? It was when you *stopped* wearing it that things started to get better. You got that job and ..." Judy stopped in mid-conversation, she was not sure whether to continue. There was another awkward pause:

"Well, go on ... what?" urged Nasra. She needed to hear all of this, sensing this was building up to something significant about to be divulged by her friend.

Judy smiled at Neil, seeking his approval before she told her friend. He nodded.

"I'm pregnant ... after years of trying!"

This was totally unexpected, Nasra's emotions quickly changing gears.

"Oh darlings!" She gave her friends a hug. "I'm so pleased for you both."

They hastily finished their drinks, their moods now very different from a few moments earlier. Nasra glanced at her watch.

"This is wonderful news, and we must talk some more, but I have to be up bright an early tomorrow. It's time I was heading off. But hey, you two, keep doing what you are doing. Old necklaces, relics – whatever it is you've done ... it seems to be working for you!"

Nasra departed. It was so good to hear this happy news right at the end of the evening. They would make good parents she was sure. As she drove south towards her home, all the other things they had talked about were lodged in her mind as well. *Funny* she thought catching sight of the bracelet she herself was wearing. *Forgotten I had even put that on tonight!*

Neil and Judy decided to spend a little longer together in the pub. Shortly afterwards, however, they found themselves loyally recalling their memories of those innocent days of now well over a decade ago, from the back of a cab as they travelled home.

7. Late Night Drama

Nasra was half way home before she realised; she had left her phone behind. *Damn,* she thought. There was no alternative, she would have to go back. Quickly looking in her rear view mirror she pulled over to the inside lane ready to take the roundabout ahead. If she was quick there would at least be some chance of reclaiming it tonight.

She grabbed her bag from the front seat and slammed the car door shut behind her before walking briskly across the car park and through the same doorway she had exited fifteen minutes earlier. *What a stupid thing to do.* As smart phones go it wasn't the most desirable, hopefully she would be in luck. She stopped in the entrance, not wishing to appear conspicuous. Looking across at the table where they had been sitting gave her the answer she didn't want. The table was empty. It was very unlikely that anyone one else would have come and gone from there in such a short space of time. A man from a nearby table was throwing her a look, and the couple that were sitting adjacent to where she and her friends had been were looking up too. She shouldn't stand here staring; she was now drawing unnecessary attention to herself. *The Barman,* she thought, starting to move forward towards the central bar. The area was crowded, mainly with men getting their last orders in. It was much busier now than thirty minutes or so earlier. This was typical – she was in a hurry and getting the attention of the guy behind the bar was going to be difficult.

"Excuse me." No response. She raised her hand,

accidentally brushing against the man standing on front of her.

"Excuse me." Nasra repeated. The barman looked up whilst he continued to pour out a pint of Guinness, but he still didn't respond through the surrounding noise. Nasra felt an unwelcome glow start to fill her cheeks. All she wanted to do was ask him something.

Just then, the large elderly man who had clocked her from his seat when she stood in the doorway came up and stood beside her. He could see she was anxious about something.

"Oi, Barry!" He shouted, leaning across the bar and addressing the barman. "Have a word with the lady can you?" He flicked his thumb to his right where Nasra stood. The barman came over, rubbing his hands on a towel. Nasra nodded a quick smile of appreciation as the large man stood grinning like a Cheshire cat.

"I'm sorry, but I was sitting over there a while ago and I left my phone on the table. I don't suppose you've seen it?" Her question was greeted with an unnerving moment of silence by the barman who continued to rub his hands dry before answering her.

"Well, you might be in luck." He paused again.

What sort of answer was that? Had he got the phone?

"You know the couple you were with don't you?"

Nasra was puzzled. She glanced at the man to her left that was still standing there grinning like a Cheshire cat, and clinging on to every word of the conversation between her and the barman.

"Well, yes." She replied rather sheepishly.

"Reckon you're in luck then. No one has handed anything in and no one else has been over there. Most likely they took it for you." The barman smiled and turned away to carry on serving the noisy crowd.

"There you go." Said the large man to her left. "All will be well."

Nasra flicked her lips nervously upwards as she briefly thanked him for helping to get the barman's attention. He gently touched her arm as she turned away.

"That's alright. Now, no rush I'm sure. Let me buy you a drink."

This was the last thing she wanted right now and not the way she would generally choose to acquaint herself with any man.

"Oh no, really, it is kind of you but I have to be somewhere."

The man smiled, he didn't try and persuade her any further.

Seconds later Nasra was driving down Lincoln Road towards town. She would take a right at the first roundabout and once she had crossed under the parkway the second roundabout would lead her onto the ring road that circled Bretton. Annoyed at causing herself this trouble, she then had another thought: *They were taking a cab.* She hoped they were already home otherwise she would have to sit and wait in the car. The journey to her friend's house would only take a few minutes – six or seven at most.

She was only a few hundred yards from Neil and Judy's home, the night was clear and the street lamps provided good illumination, so she was quite sure that the figure she could see walking at the side of the road was Neil! He was striding briskly in a direction that would take him *away* from his house. He had his phone in his hand and hood pulled up over his head. He didn't look up. This was odd, he'd hardly had time to get home, so where was he going this time of night? But that was only the part of it. As Nasra slowed the car she saw something was hanging from his neck, something rather old and ancient-looking. They had just spent two hours together talking in great detail about the necklace thing and how he has now detached himself from it . . . so what was it doing hanging from his neck?

Nasra pulled her Nissan Micra into a lay-by that was actually a bus stop. She needed a moment to think. She had just seen her best friend's husband out doing something he had just gone to great lengths to denounce. Judy wouldn't know about this; he must be deceiving her. Nasra's heart sank. She felt an uncomfortable chill work its way down her spine. How could he still be wearing that thing after all they had said? She was going to have to get her phone and see what Judy had to say, but tonight wasn't going to be the right time to get into any more discussions. Letting out a sigh, she pulled clear of the lay-by to complete the last hundred yards of her journey.

Judy opened the door almost as soon as Nasra had knocked. Was she surprised to see her? Nasra wasn't sure. Her friend rubbed her eyes, deliberately keeping them from meeting Nasra's.

"I left my phone, the barman said you might have picked it up."

Judy sat in the living room looking straight ahead. She didn't answer.

"What's happened? You're upset. Where's Neil?" She wasn't expecting Judy to answer the last question first, but she turned, now fixing her rubbed-red eyes firmly upon Nasra's.

"He's gone out ... bloody gone out now ... this time of night – when we had only just got in." Her anger was obvious.

"Oh Sweetie, come here." Nasra moved close to give her a hug. Judy continued to sniffle.

"As soon as we got in the car he started getting messages. After a few minutes I asked him who it was, and ... he just ..." Judy burst into tears, and Nasra held her close, looking across the room towards the window, wondering what Neil was thinking right now.

So she doesn't know about the necklace then. Now her task was to comfort Judy. As she looked down she saw the life growing inside her friend. The bulge was noticeable now that she knew, but even at what was nearly the halfway stage of her pregnancy Judy's slender frame visually gave little away.

"I'm sure he won't be long," Nasra said, "sometimes guys need space, he's been cooped up with us two all night." Nasra was trying but it wasn't working. There was no conviction in her voice. She didn't believe in what she was saying and she sensed that Judy didn't either. Words from earlier that evening started to echo in her mind. *'I still wore that old necklace though, at least – it was the last thing to go.'* Clearly it *hadn't* gone! And what was it that Judy said so emphatically? *'It was when you stopped wearing it that things started to get better.'*

Suddenly, Judy gave out a cry and put her hand to her side.

Nasra felt it. She felt the pain reverberate through Judy and into her own body. She felt something else as well, something bad. The bracelet she wore now didn't shine, something was overpowering it ... and it wasn't good.

"My God, Judy!" Nasra released her grip in response to her friend's reaction, but then Judy let out another wail.

The necklace, it was a bad omen. From everything they had both told her earlier that evening, right from years ago when Neil started wearing it, bad things have happened ... and he was *still* wearing it now!

"I'm ringing an ambulance" Nasra reached desperately for her bag and scrambled for her phone, but of course, it wasn't there.

"On the side – I picked it up." Gasped Judy, pointing with her other hand as she doubled over on the chair in agony. Nasra grabbed her phone with one hand, the other still holding Judy's. She called an ambulance. As soon as she was done she rang Neil on Judy's phone. There was no answer so she sent a text.

A blue light in the distance was the first sign. He broke into a jog – then he ran. The confirmation was seeing their friend's car on the roadside, accompanied by an ambulance. Neil returned just in time, he hadn't even looked at his phone the last few minutes. He burst in through the back door.

"Judy, Judy!" He screamed. "What's happened? The baby . . . is the baby alright?"

Nasra rose to her feet and gently placed a hand on Neil's shoulder in an attempt to calm him.

"She's in good hands Neil. They are taking her to hospital. You go in the ambulance and I will follow." She hadn't answered his question, she couldn't. Neil stood for a second, his legs astride and his arms slightly away from his sides, like a man ready to fight but no one to challenge. His jaw fell slightly ajar but no words could flow from his mouth. After a moment or two he darted forward, leaned over, and hugged his wife as the two paramedics proceeded to haul her into the back of the ambulance.

"It's going to be alright, I promise," he said, blinking rapidly as moisture formed somewhere deep within his eyes.

8. Four Drunken Men

Peterborough: June 2014

For Nasra the weeks had rolled slowly by but now, at last summer had come. She found herself one evening sitting at the table in her living room staring at the puzzle in front of her. It had been on the go for weeks and she still hadn't finished it. Things hadn't been good for her the last few weeks; there had been the old man – Mr Griggs who had suddenly passed away, then she had needed to get lifts and pay for a cab for a few days while her car was being fixed. This was a pain and had cost her extra money she hadn't got. Her mind wandered from the puzzle that lay in front of her and she started to think about her friends again. This was leading her round in circles and she felt so guilty. Letting out a sigh she rose from the table and wandered into the kitchen, stopping at the doorway as the sight of a heap of dishes on the drainer reminded her of her next task. Shuffling unenthusiastically across the kitchen she turned on the hot tap and started to fill the bowl.

'I haven't spoken to Judy for nearly two weeks' she murmured aloud to herself. *Still don't know if she knows.* Nasra hadn't told Judy about what she had seen that night. The few days following had been quite upsetting and it had gone from her mind. Now, recalling that she had seen Neil out late that night wearing the necklace he said he doesn't wear any more made her feel guilty, because she hadn't had the chance to confront him about it. What was he really about? Could that old relic really still be affecting the way he was behaving?

She rolled up her sleeves, pausing for a minute as she unclipped the bracelet from her wrist. *The bracelet* she thought. *Hasn't brought me so much luck just lately.* But then, another thought entered her head as she dragged the first few plates and cups into the warm soap-sudsed water. *At least they didn't lose the baby.* That night when they got home from the pub they had all thought Judy had a miscarriage. She rested, and by the next morning felt much better, the pain she had felt had been caused by something else entirely. This was all good, Neil and Judy would have been devastated if it had happened again.

Nasra finished the last few dishes then wandered back into the living room. With her hands on her hips she stared at the puzzle that lay in front of her. *Time only ever stands still in a picture* she thought to herself, looking at the completed sepia-toned section that depicted a scene of the main street of the City at around the turn of the century. There were people, buildings, and snapshots of urban greenery making up the other surrounding scenes, and in the middle was The Cathedral.

Nasra had never noticed until now just how striking the building was. Now, it grabbed her interest as its nobility seemed to stand out. She had never actually been inside the building but had heard a lot about its past. *I bet it would have a tale or two to tell* she thought. She'd had the puzzle laid out for weeks now, she so much wanted to complete it, but the final piece was missing.

✿ ✿ ✿ ✿ ✿

For Judy, time had passed slowly. Her slender frame bulged slightly larger with each passing day, it hadn't been the smoothest of pregnancies. There had been the morning sickness, the overwhelming tiredness and inevitable irritability, and the occasional argument with Neil when she'd felt he'd come up short of the mark. But all in all things were moving in the right direction.

All was fine until one Sunday night when Judy found herself sitting in her kitchen constantly checking the clock. She couldn't go to bed, she was totally unable to relax; her mind was fervent with worry and her brain conjuring up all sorts of crazy scenarios: Perhaps he'd had an accident and the police were going to knock at the door any minute ... how would she cope with that? She couldn't bear to dwell on it, but right now she was unable to prevent herself from doing so. What if he'd got drunk and found another woman ... and he wasn't coming back at all tonight?

Stop it! She said to herself. This was madness. He was late, he should have been in by now but it wasn't crisis time yet, surely! Of course not, what was she thinking. He'd probably just overrun slightly – misjudging the time with the lads on their night out. Yes, that's all it would be, soon he'd be home and she could relax. With immense mental effort she convinced herself that bed was the best place for her. He had a key, and there was no obligation for her to stay up stupidly late in her fragile state.

❊ ❊ ❊ ❊ ❊

Just a mile or two away in the city centre, right outside a crowded bar, four men staggered aimlessly in the street talking loudly in drunken slurs.

"Time to make a move ... my mates." Neil attempted to slap an arm around the shoulders of each of his mates as he blurted out the barely comprehensible phrases. He missed his target with two of them and the inevitable result was an attempt by the others to do likewise. So, shortly, four drunken men in their twenties were roaming a city centre street in a *sort of* arm in arm fashion, lurching first one way then the other.

Paddy spoke:

"We are the boys ... you are my mates right? I see you in work tomorrow."

Paddy was drunk, but a tiny portion of his brain reminded him that this was a Sunday night and that they actually all had work tomorrow – and at the same place! However inebriated he and the others were he felt this piece of information needed to be passed on by way of a warning.

"You wor' ... worry too much mate ... we'll be fine."

"I see yous all in the morning." Jimmy then started staggering off in a completely different direction of his own.

"No, wait," called Neil, "we need to stay together, we need to supperot ... to suplort ... support each other." (He was barely able to get the words out!)

The foursome staggered on towards the town square. It was then that Neil had the bright idea of taking a short cut.

"Hey guys, follow me." With exaggerated beckoning arm gestures, he attempted to guide his three mates under an archway. "We can go through here ... we can get a taxi ..."

"Cabs don't drive through here mate. This ain't a taxi place ... I mean ... this ain't a road." Jimmy's eyes were trying to focus. Where were they? Now, just barely able to recognise the large illuminated building that loomed over them with its illusive sway from left to right, Jimmy attempted to explain:

"This is the cathdrol ... the ... catherole ... the ..." his voice tailed off as he let out an almighty belch that was greeted by uncontrollable raucous laughter from the others. The heavy ancient wooden doors that usually close off the area at night had unintentionally been left open on this occasion, allowing the unruly crowd to walk straight through into the Cathedral precincts.

It was as the group managed to painfully work out with collective effort that the route they actually needed to take was off to the left, passing in front of the majestic building, that things started to happen:

Firstly, Joey, (probably the one out of the four of them who was the most paralytically out of it), pointed towards the trees beyond a small wall about fifty metres away;

"There ... who's that?" He tried to focus his glazed eyes on a dark shape that he thought he could see. As he peered more intently, still squinting, it became evident to him that the dark shape he thought he'd just seen simply wasn't there!

"You're stupid man ... out of it man." Paddy wasn't having any of it.

They carried on towards the gateway that led to a small winding stretch of road. Neil had convinced the other three this was the best place to get a taxi from. He may have been a little drunk but he knew where the cabs would line up, surely they needed to head through the gateway over to the left. All of them were now just larking about; Joey's comments had started something and now, all of a sudden they were seeing one thing or other lurking behind a bush, or in the shadows by the wall.

Then, Neil stopped dead in his tracks. This was different, there was something moving about. He tried to focus on the patch of grass beside the north-facing wall of the Cathedral. What little light there was still seemed to blur everything and dazzle him. He swayed, trying desperately to keep his balance. His brain, now desperately compounding every possible sobering signal it was receiving, was trying to make sense of what his eyes were seeing. Frantically pacing around in front of him, first one way the another was someone in a dark robe. His hands were placed behind his back. Neil had dropped back from the group who were now calling to him as they moved towards the exit from the Cathedral grounds. For a moment he stood transfixed, there *was* someone there. Neil looked up. He staggered as he planted his left foot in an effort to change direction, then, he moved hastily to catch up with the others. Seconds later he caught up with the rest, and, almost completely having forgotten what he had just seen, he felt fully returned to his full state of drunkenness.

❧ ❧ ❧ ❧ ❧

Words between Judy and Neil some thirty minutes later were few and far between. She hadn't waited up, but neither had she managed to sleep. Although rather annoyed with her other half, it was obvious that he was not operating in comprehensible conversation mode so it was probably best to leave any attempt to discuss matters until the morning, however cross or upset she might feel. The trouble for Neil was his brain was in a sort of overdrive. As his head hit the pillow with a soft thud, images from the room started to form patterns in his mind: Dark shapes moved vertically across his vision, and the doorway cascaded in a never-ending loop.

The alcohol may have severely impaired his judgement but it did not stop him from sleeping, and it did not stop him dreaming either. When he awoke the next morning, there was little else on his mind.

9. What Neil Saw

The next day at work didn't go well. Joey had rather blown their cover by coming in late and Bob Hodgkinson, their immediate supervisor, sent him home as a disciplinary procedure for being in an unfit state to carry out his duties in a place of work. It didn't escape his notice either that the other three seemed well below par. Shortly before lunch time he made his observations clear to the remaining three of them stating in no uncertain terms that he did not ever want to see a repeat of this behaviour and suggested that perhaps a Saturday night rather than Sunday might be a better timed outlet for their wild antics in the future. So, when lunchtime came, it was not surprising that all three of them were a little down beat to say the least.

"Bit crazy last night weren't we?" remarked Paddy. The others all gave him the same look, chins on hands, their faces displaying false smiles.

"Can't do that again." Jimmy shook his head, looking down at the floor. He sounded quite definite. "All that stuff about seeing ghosts by the Cathedral eh!"

"Ah, that was all rubbish mate ... alcohol talking, Joey always gets like that when he's off his head."

Neil's eyes panned the room, the response from his colleagues left him feeling a bit uneasy. He saw something last night that they hadn't seen. His mates were referring to the other stuff ... but that was just pranks. And, this morning, when he had woken up it felt weird. He'd expected the headache, but he'd also had some authentically realistic nightmare about something ... but what? It is so annoying – that feeling of apparent surety when you've just had a strong dream, full of images and words that are startlingly clear and easy to remember ... for about twenty seconds! By the time he got himself downstairs for breakfast and wanted to put things into words to tell Judy, the memory of the detail was about as clear as thick smoke! What Neil did remember was that he'd had a dream – and he just felt that it was important. There was something powerful about it – as if he was being pulled towards some place or some thing. At this point he felt he had to say something.

"Well, you might say it's all rubbish, but I saw something last night too, when you lot were up ahead."

The other two looked at him, and Paddy, clocking Neil's vacant gaze started to smirk.

"No, listen. I know we were all a bit out of it but I swear there *was* someone there, over by the wall."

The others looked straight at Neil as an uneasy silence filled the room.

"Here we go," muttered Paddy under his breath staring down at the floor, "Mr. supernatural himself dishes out the next instalment. What is it this time – some ancient dude from years ago prancing around and you're going to tell us all about him, what he did, where he lived – and it's all going to turn out to be true?"

Neil's mouth fell open and his head dropped, he couldn't make eye contact. Paddy's remark had stopped him in his tracks, this was hopeless and so unfair; it had a ring of truth about it that just made things worse; no one was going to take him seriously – he knew it. Neil didn't say any more about it to his two mates that day.

When he got home that evening there was still only one thing on his mind. Over dinner he told Judy what he remembered of his dream:

"The first thing ... it was cold and gloomy, but still daytime I think. I recall sitting and talking quietly around a solid wooden table in some large old, cold room. We were sharing a meal ... and I think there was a small fire in the corner. I was holding some plants that I must have gathered ... probably herbs of some sort – but I don't remember picking them. There were others there too. It's all a bit mixed up, but it feels like it was a long, long time ago."

Judy listened to her husband's testimony noting the look of anxiety in his face. She opened her mouth to speak, but Neil hadn't finished.

"There was something else. Some place nearby . . . but I wasn't actually there. Somehow it didn't feel right. It felt like this *thing* was always there ... always keeping check. Maybe this was where I *should* have been? As if I had done something wrong and this was my punishment."

Judy could see the worry in her partner's eyes, but she wasn't sure what to say to him.

"And you couldn't really remember any of this earlier? It seems very real to you now!"

"That's just it you see. I couldn't remember anything until Paddy said something at work today. I know they were taking the mickey a bit and it sounds crazy, but it's as if I was actually there – somewhere in the past. It's like I've actually *been* to that place, it was so real."

Judy grabbed her husband's arm giving him a grin designed to comfort.

"Don't forget, you'd had a lot to drink. That might have something to do with it?"

"There's something else as well." Continued Neil, ignoring his wife. "I saw something ... by the Cathedral ... as we walked through the precincts around midnight."

Now Judy really was having doubts. Was this going to turn out to be another of his 'spooked out' experiences? Hadn't he said earlier they all reckoned they'd seen a ghost? Judy laughed gently, hoping that making light of the whole situation was now perhaps the best line of tact to take but, again Neil spoke before she could respond. He stood up and started to stride around the room.

"You don't understand. You see, I'm positive the big thing I felt looming behind me – it *was* the Cathedral."

Judy stared at her husband, her mouth half open, not getting what he was driving at.

"Don't you see?" continued Neil, his eyes now darting from side to side as if he was frantically trying to work something out as he paced round in circles. "The ghost I saw ... it was like he could be the person *I* was feeling in *my* dream!"

10. Festival Day

The weather stayed warm for the rest of that week, and the following weekend was the *Peterborough Festival,* an event that had stamped its place on the local calendar over the last few years. There were various events taking place around the city: a vintage car parade, displays in the town square, but the main action took place in the town park to the north of the City centre. Neil, Judy and Nasra had decided to make a day of it.

The two women had lunched together in town then walked on up to the park where they had made a base for the afternoon.

"It's absolutely stifling," Judy said, adjusting the blanket she had brought to place against the grassy bank in an effort to get herself comfortable. Nasra raised her sun-glasses a little and smiled in her direction.

"Have you got enough cream on those arms?" Her friend nodded and shut her eyes, resting her head against the angle of the slope and managing to get herself a little more settled.

"Yes, I'm alright – would just like to lie here and listen to the music for a while." Judy lay back and let the sun do its work. Nasra sat on the grassy bank, tapping her sandalled foot to the rhythm of the jazz music emanating from a distance of about thirty yards in front of them. People were walking past, some stopping to listen, but it didn't spoil their view of the band as they had positioned themselves a little way up the bank. It was quite uplifting to hear the sharp sounds reverberate through the early summer air.

"This is pretty cool. So many people, so much going on ... so much colour ... and *vivacity!*" Judy cocked her head and grinned at her friend.

"Vivacity, hah!" She said. Nasra's remark was a light-hearted dig; *Vivacity* is the name of the local council's art, entertainment and sports organisational branch, responsible for the implementation of many of the communal facilities to aid such events as the festival.

As they relaxed there on the lush green grass Judy had something on her mind. She started to tell her friend about the conversation she'd had with Neil a few days earlier. She was bothered by the dreams her husband had been experiencing.

"I mean, he feels it's like he is being watched all the time." She said. "It's certainly bothering him."

"Sounds odd, but it is only a dream we are talking about here. Let's not get too carried away."

"But it's what he said happened in those dreams," Judy continued.

"Go on," urged her friend.

"They always seem to happen long ago – like hundreds of years, and he says something about being part of a group."

This was just starting to get interesting when Nasra's attention was diverted towards an approaching figure – a large dark-skinned man who looked a little unsteady on his feet. Her eyes tracked him as he came closer. He was clutching leaflets in both hands as he staggered up onto the side of the bank about ten yards from where they sat.

"Oh no!" Giggled Nasra, nodding to the right as she pulled her glasses adrift of her face. Judy, interested, lifted her head and followed her friend's gaze.

"He'd better not be coming to preach to *us*," she muttered quietly, but it was too late. The intended targets – a young couple to their right, had already waved him on. Now, as he wobbled his way forward, his face beamed up at the two women.

"Hey ... how you doin' ladies? He began in what sounded like a slight West Indian accent. "I would jus' like to take a few mooments to tell ya' 'bout our community."

"Well ... okay –"

"Mi name is Gladiolus Acoufonte, but ya' can call mi *Gladstone.*"

The two women gave each other a nervous glance as *Gladstone* continued to tell them all about the Caribbean culture and its importance of ethnicity within the City. All the time he was doing this he prodded the leaflet on top of the pile repeatedly as if it displayed unarguable proof of what he was telling them. Nasra and Judy were both finding it hard to take him seriously and stop themselves from exploding with laughter.

After a few minutes of mainly one way conversation that was greeted with nothing more than the odd smile, and grunt of approval, the large man moved on, thanking them for their time, just about managing to stay on his feet as he negotiated the downward slope of the bank. Once he had disappeared, the two women burst into laughter before coming to grips with themselves and turning their minds back to the present.

"I wonder where he's got to?" Said Judy presently, referring to her husband. Nasra had been thinking the same thing. Had Neil gone straight back to the car or had he got distracted – talking to someone perhaps, or making a call? *A call he wouldn't want Judy to hear no doubt*, thought Nasra to herself, as she started to dwell on the situation. *I mean, like where is he? It shouldn't be taking him this long to park up and walk back to here to be with us.*

Nasra still hadn't told Judy about seeing Neil out on that night a few weeks ago wearing the necklace he had led them to believe he had got rid of. Surely now that he wasn't present, this would be a good time? But then Judy's face changed as she scrambled to her feet, waving her arms.

"We're over here." She called, as her husband peered towards them from the distance.

"I think he's seen us." Commented Nasra as he came closer.

"You were a long flipping time!" Judy was not impressed. Neil merely grunted, wearing a vacant expression that didn't quite fit with the mood. Nasra was keen to defuse the tension. *Maybe it's time for refreshments?* She thought.

"Let's go and get us something to drink," Nasra said, seeing that Neil looked very much like he could do with one.

"I can't believe I've finally done it." Neil said, gazing straight ahead towards the jazz band that had just struck up the familiar opening riff of *'Oh When The Saints go marching in'*. Judy frowned.

"And I can't believe parking the car could prove so difficult either. What do you want ... a blinking medal?" There was bitterness in her tone, and now, Neil was going to ignore her, Nasra could sense it.

"Hey," she said, giving Judy a nudge in the ribs. "Tell him about Gladstone."

The mood changed as the two women recounted the amusing story of a few minutes previously. Their giggle turned to laughs as they described the way he had wobbled along, obviously quite drunk. Neil looked at them both but didn't seem to appreciate the humour of the moment. *Suppose you had to be there,* Nasra thought.

"Come on, lets go and get that drink" she said.

"Drink?" Shrieked Judy, her face now creased with laughter. "If we go to the bar we might meet Gladstone. I bet I can wobble better than him ... look." Judy started to exaggerate what was for her already the quite arduous effort of walking. The two women burst out into an almost uncontrollable fit of laughter as she did so.

"This guy I met ... on my way back, he was all dressed up." (Neil seemed pre-occupied with telling them about something that had happened on his way back to the car.)

"Dressed up? We are about the only people who aren't!"

He really didn't seem to get what the day was about. If there wasn't something happening right in front of you, then it would be going on in another corner. Nasra looked around her and for the first time that day took in the diversity of the moment. This wasn't a bad city to live in at all. There is actually quite a bit going on culturally if you look around. Her own culture was well represented and she was proud of that.

"Suppose that counts as quite a big moment really ... I mean, it's like a landmark" Neil's dreamy voice droned on but his words paled into insignificance becoming part of the background noise. Judy was still doing 'the walk', it really was quite funny. Nasra couldn't help laughing. Why couldn't Neil at least manage to have a bit of a laugh instead of rattling on about seeing someone dressed up ... as if he was the only one!

The two women looked at Neil as their laughter subsided. His eyes were wide-open but there was something about his expression. *He seems a bit distant, better ask him what he is on about.* Nasra turned to face Neil.

"You said someone was *'dressed up'*?"

Neil turned to look at her as if slightly taken by surprise that she was finally asking him.

"Yeah, and I gave it to him – just seemed like the right moment."

Judy stopped laughing and the two women looked first at each other then at him, slightly puzzled:

"What right moment ... what are you on about?" enquired his other half emphatically.

"That thing ... we were talking about the other week ... how our luck turned – remember?"

Neil was trying desperately to stimulate their memories to recall the importance they had all attached to this that night in the pub several weeks ago, but right now neither woman was on his wavelength.

He couldn't seriously be saying that now, today he had just

given that old necklace away ... to some bloke in the park? After all that had happened to them! Nasra felt that if she was in Judy's shoes she would be livid if she found out he still had it in his possession.

"No, no, seriously," began Nasra, deciding it was time to show some respect and at least hear Neil out. "There have been lots of folk dressed up in the park today. *Who* did you give *what* to?"

"That old necklace. I gave it away because he just seemed to be ..."

So he has been stupid enough to ... "Go on ... what?" Judy wasn't happy.

"He just seemed to be ... like the right person to give it to. I don't know – maybe because of his costume?" Neil scanned their puzzled angry faces before continuing: "Well ... a monk, alright? You know ... give an ancient thing to an ancient bloke ... it just seemed right. Get it?" They didn't.

"You've given that old necklace thing to some stranger dressed as a monk? In the town park ... *today?*" Judy raised her voice. As Nasra had predicted, this was not going down well.

"No, no, you don't understand. It *wasn't* here in the town park, it was on my way back to the car park, on the footpath behind the Cathedral. It was all a bit odd really."

Suddenly they were listening.

"There was this bloke dressed as a monk, he asked if he could help me. Well, I wondered what he meant and why he was asking, but then it clicked, and in a moment of inspiration I thought, yes – take it! So I gave him the necklace."

Nasra looked first at Neil then at Judy and then back at Neil, she was gobsmacked.

"So you got rid of it once and for all ... today?" Nasra frowned, her bottom lip parted from her top one.

"Seemed like he didn't want it though; in fact, his reaction was a bit strange. When he took it from my hand he looked like death warmed up ... like what I had given him was some sort of curse!"

Judy stared at her husband. She thought he had got rid of the necklace ages ago.

"You said it was the last thing to go, but you still had it here, today? How many more times have you been wearing it behind my back?" Judy was angry now.

Neil screwed up his face. Why wasn't she just pleased that he had got rid of it?

"And another thing," Judy continued, as Nasra's eyes spoke with a look that begged her not to continue, "makes me think what else you might be doing behind my back." Nasra looked at Neil who was now clearly upset by that last remark. She needed to say something before this became embarrassing, but there was no chance as Neil replied:

"Oh, that's rich ... so you don't trust me now?"

"Well, all I'm saying is you are always off out ... some deal or other ... got to meet this bloke or that bloke or some other."

Don't say any more Judy Nasra thought to herself, but it was too late. This was hitting where it hurts. Neil muttered some expletives, put his hands in his pocket, turned his back and walked off.

"So off he goes," (she deliberately raised her voice for this last remark), "You just go dear ... don't worry about me, Nasra and I will find our own way home."

This wasn't good. Nasra felt she had been disloyal towards her friend. After all, she had known he still had the old necklace the night when she saw him out wearing it, and she had not told Judy then or at any time since. What good would it have done? It was up to them what they decided to tell each other – none of her business really. Surely it was best to let things run their course? But now Judy was quite worked up, her partner had stormed off, and there were clearly some elements of mistrust between the two of them. This wasn't good.

Nasra couldn't leave it like this, she had to do something:

"I'm sure he will calm down" she said as Judy began to gather up their things, "This isn't the first time he's stormed off and I'm sure it won't be the last –"

"Oh! You're sure are you?" Her friend cut in.

"Well, I mean ... him going off ... out – to do stuff. He does this ... right?"

Judy thrust a drink bottle firmly into the picnic bag without acknowledging her friend's last remark. This was going to be difficult, but now he'd upset Judy by quite nonchalantly declaring what he had done, and then storming off again, Nasra felt she would have to come clean.

The two women walked off through the park at Judy's pace, it was Nasra who had to make the effort to keep up.

"He has been out wearing it – the necklace, he should have told you. It's not good enough to say you are going to do one thing and then not follow it through."

"Oh, right. That's nice to know." There was a distinct air of sarcasm in the tone of Judy's reply.

"I don't know how he can just casually announce that he has just given it away today when we thought he had already got rid of it ... from what he said – that night in the pub." Judy's eyes were set in a glare straight ahead of her. She was walking faster than was good for her in her current state, and she chose not to reply to her friend. This was getting to be awkward, but the guy was obviously up to something behind the scenes, and Judy was her friend.

"I saw him out wearing the necklace – that night we met in *The Paul Pry* and I had to come back to yours to get my phone. He was striding along the Bretton ring-road, as if he had to get to somewhere, fast."

Judy stopped and faced her friend.

"Oh he was, was he? And I suppose that makes him a bad guy does it? Because I was at home, nearly having a miscarriage?"

"No, he's not a bad guy, I just thought I needed to tell you –"

"*You* needed to tell *me*? Five weeks later? Because what he told us today suddenly made you think did it Nasra?"

This wasn't expected. Why was she being so tetchy? Surely she could see that this had to be said.

"Look, Judy," Nasra tried to comfort her friend by gripping her arms, but Judy flinched in refusal. "I'm sorry, I didn't mean ... I just think you need to ask him what he is up to –"

"Stop!" She raised a hand. "Leave it girl. You're going too deep with this."

"But, I wanted to tell you because –"

"Get the hint friend, you're out of order. Neil is my guy and we are good. This is no big deal and we don't need you sticking your nose in any more." Judy walked on.

Nasra stood rooted to the spot. She was shocked and hurt, but, thinking quickly, she could at least drive her friend home. Maybe they could talk? But when the offer was made it was refused. Judy just raised her hand again and said she thought it best on this occasion if she took the bus. The two women, both feeling quite low, went their separate ways.

11. A Slip through Time

An hour later Nasra sat in her living room with her head in her hands. She had left the park on her own late that afternoon feeling very low. How had it got to this? All she had wanted to do was open Judy's eyes to her husbands behaviour, but as far as Judy was concerned her eyes were perfectly capable of seeing what was happening around her, and she didn't appreciate what had sounded to her like criticism. This was all so silly, and it had ended up with all three of them going their separate ways.

Before driving home Nasra had sent a text apology. She scrolled her phone to see if there had been a reply but there hadn't. *I can't leave it like this* she thought, so, hauling herself up from the seat she sent another text while she began pacing around the room.

Time passed and it was horrible, it wasn't meant to happen like this. Why hadn't she warned Judy earlier that Neil still had this blasted thing? And why was it such a big deal anyway? Now all three of them seemed alienated from each other, because they had all let something quite silly get to them. Then there was Neil; where was he right now? He had left the scene first. *Probably went back to get his car and drove home. They are most likely together now, and made up.*

As she gazed across the room Nasra caught sight of the clock, it was past six! She decided that the last thing she wanted to do was prepare a meal, so a takeaway it was to be.

As Nasra turned the key in the ignition of her silver Micra, she was just glad to get out of her flat. She brought herself fish and chips and ate them out of the wrapper in her car outside in the parking bay. Just as she was finishing the last few scraps her phone buzzed. Almost tipping the chip paper and its remnants onto the seat of her car, she scrambled to see the message. It was Judy at last replying to her apologetic texts. It simply read; *'Okay. I'm sorry too'.*

Nasra screwed up her meal wrappers and shoved them into a plastic bag she kept in the front pouch. Tying it into a knot she opened the car windows to let some air in. A few minutes later she found herself heading out of town driving in no particular direction. She often did this when something was on her mind; one time about a year ago when her mum had told her that her uncle was terminally ill, she got in her car and drove a fifty mile round trip into Leicestershire and back, just to clear her mind of the shock. Sometimes she had to get away and driving around on a summer evening was a release for her.

As she drove, her mind wandered. Gazing ahead at her own hands on the steering wheel she was once more reminded of the bracelet she herself was wearing. Why did she feel she now always had to wear it? After all it had only been a gift from a casual elderly acquaintance! Surely this was all a bit silly? And the dreams ... what was it about those dreams? As she thought deeper she felt questions growing within her mind, quietly working their way to the surface. Were there links? Neil had been having some pretty powerful dreams too, and hadn't this all started months ago when his workmates reckoned he'd got some 'second sight' of things to come? And in her own dreams: she always seemed to be in control, as if the people around looked to her for guidance or to solve a problem. The further she drove the deeper she thought. Perhaps it was all meant to mean something.

Synapses in her brain made sudden connections as her mind dug deep to remember something her father had told her many years previously. There had been a time when he was sure something had guided him to a right decision. He'd been driving along the busy city ring road and the car in front looked a touch unsteady, as if the driver wasn't really in control. He'd wanted to overtake but felt unsure of doing so in case the driver was to swerve into him or something like. Suddenly he remembered a dream or a moment from a daydream, imagination, call it what you will. He visualised himself overtaking another vehicle – speeding past and looking back feeling relieved. Had he won a race? Had he avoided danger? The situation wasn't clear. All he ever said about it was that he knew he had to act and overtake in that split second. What actually happened next was chilling; once he'd got a hundred metres or so past the vehicle, he saw in his rear view mirror that it did indeed swerve off into the central reservation and end up at right angles to the oncoming traffic. The miracle was that no other traffic was close by, and the driver got out unhurt, apparently having just fallen asleep! What might have occurred if he hadn't overtaken the vehicle at the exact moment he did?

Her car headlights were on, she had been driving for miles, lost in thought. Now, much later on that cool evening in early summer, as the light was fading fast she found herself heading back towards Peterborough.

The lights of the oncoming traffic flowed past as her mind, now tired, and only partly on the task in hand, allowed the imagery to drift into her subconscious. She realised she had driven back into town and was now heading out north towards Bretton. Oncoming headlights dazzled her as now she became aware she was actually not far from Neil and Judy's estate. Passing a wooded area to her left immediately came a vision, flooding her mind; it was so real, she was walking in a woods, a long time ago gathering plants – was she looking for something? She wasn't quite sure.

Brightness flickered all around her like a beacon, no longer just the light of oncoming traffic. Now there was rain in the air too. Instinctively she turned on the windscreen wipers, then, dazzling headlights through an intermittently partially clear rain-sprayed windscreen became like watching an old movie, the strobe-like effect simulating the archaic footage – it was as if it was being projected all around – just for her!

Suddenly she became alert. Through the flickers, there was a figure standing motionless. Slowing her vehicle she could see who it was, but surely not! This couldn't be!

"Neil?" She stopped and wound down the window.

"Neil?" the figure didn't answer, he stood gazing straight ahead. The rain now pounded in heavy spats against her face and the wind had grown much stronger.

"Get in, I'll run you back home," she said.

He climbed into the passenger's seat, still he stared blankly straight ahead. Nasra felt her breathing start to quicken as her hand moved the gear lever in and out of position, her clutch foot depressed to the floor. What on earth was he doing out here? She glanced across at the bedraggled figure, not really sure what to make of him at all.

"What are you doing out here in the rain?" He didn't reply. Nasra paused for a moment, she lifted her foot slowly while peering into the mirror, now forcing herself to concentrate on pulling away. Then she tried again; "Look, if something's the matter I'm sure we can sort it out." She looked away from the wheel across at Neil. His face was pale and expressionless it was as if he'd had some sort of breakdown.

She managed to refocus her attention on the road in front, unintentionally tightening her grip on the steering wheel as she did so. Sweat oozed from every gland as a shudder ran down her spine. *What is the matter with him? Why won't he speak?* For a second or two she couldn't remember anything, her mind was now locked into a memory battle she couldn't win. Where was she going? There was only a moment to dwell on this before something else kicked in – the car ... now she couldn't stop it from accelerating! And it was heading towards the roundabout!

"What the ..." Nasra couldn't get the words out, every drop of her concentration was now being sapped by the demands of what lay in front of her. The roundabout was now very close, she would have to take it at speed. Thank God there was nothing coming. She certainly wouldn't have been able to stop if there had been!

Seconds later they were at the slip road leading onto the A47 going away from Bretton. The rain beat down and the groaning wipers did their best, but Nasra clearly no longer had complete control over her vehicle.

"Neil ... *Neil!* What's going on?" she shrieked. Still he didn't speak, he just sat staring straight ahead. Nasra's brain told her something else; *What is he wearing? His coat is unusually long, and thick material to be wearing for this time of year, and what is that hoodie thing covering his entire head for?* It made him look quite odd, she'd never seen him like this before. Her thoughts scrambled, she could focus on nothing now.

Her Nissan Micra screamed down the parkway, forced, it

seemed, to overtake everything in its path. The next roundabout was fast approaching and the vehicle would not slow down. Nasra screamed, the lights of another vehicle on the roundabout were almost upon her. Instinctively she shut her eyes and her hands left the wheel to protect her face as the tyres screeched, and then ... suddenly ... everywhere was black.

Nasra opened her eyes, the realisation that nothing had actually happened flooded her mind. Had she fainted? Now trembling with fear she instinctively planted both hands firmly back on the wheel with determined urgency. It was only then that she realised the car was *still* moving – her nightmare *hadn't* ended!

It was very dark now. Where were they? This was not the A47, it wasn't even a main road! In fact, it appeared they were heading down some country lane. She tried to pull together the fragmented memories of the last few minutes; surely she had crashed? But now they seemed to be heading east out towards Eye. Staring into the dark abyss, all that was visible was what her car lights were showing her of the road ahead. Nasra tried to catch her breath, her pulse still racing as her vehicle began to gradually slow. She tried to speak as the car came to a halt by itself in what seemed like the middle of nowhere, but her throat was dry and words wouldn't form. It was as if her whole being was now paralysed in a dream-like state over which she had no control, and yet, this was happening right now. The figure beside her reached for the door handle and began to climb slowly out of the car. Filled with fear and trepidation she looked as he turned back to face her. He raised an arm, and as she tried again to call out his name he pointed forward of where he was now standing. It was as if he was indicating there was some place he had to get to, or something he wanted her to do, but she didn't understand. All Nasra could do was watch as the ghostly figure she had thought to be Neil then just disappeared into the dark, north-east Peterborough landscape.

A loud tapping sound pounded through her head as Nasra opened her eyes. Dazed for a second or two, she looked around. Was this the return to some sort of reality? Now it wasn't as dark outside either.

"You alright miss?" A police officer called out as he tapped on the passenger's window. "Can you open your window for me please?" He pointed to a lay-by in front that clearly he wanted her to pull into. Shaking, she restarted the engine and slowly pulled the car a few yards forward into the lay-by.

So Nasra was okay. The police officer surmised that she had just been the victim of a stressful evening. He didn't give her the breathalyser – she didn't seem to be inebriated and he didn't have the necessary equipment anyway. Once convinced that Nasra was in a state to continue driving, and that she would be able to find her own way home, he left her to it and went on his way.

For a few moments Nasra couldn't do anything. What had just happened? *Who the hell was that guy ... surely it was Neil .. but how ...?* She couldn't work it out. She just sat alone in her car for a moment or two trying to gather her thoughts. Had it really happened? Then, her phone vibrated. Picking it up she read the text. It was from Judy. Nasra's eyes widened as she let out a gasp. She gripped her mobile phone, pulling it close to her face, not quite able to take in the words it displayed. Any slight recovery from the trauma of the last few minutes she had started to make was thrown into disarray by what it said. It simply read:

"Neil is dead . . ."

12. Only Half the Story

For a moment all Nasra could do was stare vacantly ahead in a state of shock. She read the text again. It was as if her whole world had just imploded. Her mind raced ahead going through all the possible scenarios – none of them good. Then reality got a grip of her.

'I must get to Judy,' she said to herself. The engine fired up and she pulled away, now trembling with shock. Surely Neil had just been with *her* ... in *her* car ... just a few minutes ago!

Barely able to concentrate on the task of driving through the rain now teeming down, Nasra struggled to control both her vehicle and her emotions. Shaking, like a nervous wreck, she pulled up in front of the house and dashed from the car, plundering through the torrents of rain towards the doorway of Judy and Neil's home. Judy opened the door, and Nasra, with tears now forming in her eyes leapt upon her friend, giving her the biggest, most empathetic embrace.

"I'm sorry, I'm so sorry. My lovely, whatever has happened?" Even as she spoke Nasra was already aware of an additional force – that of Judy resisting her embrace of apparent sympathy and pushing her away. Clearly the effect of shock had meant the gravity of grief had not yet hit her friend. The two women parted and looked each other in the eyes.

"What?" A confused Nasra was the first to speak.

"Nasra, whatever is the matter?" Judy's words were

breathless, but it was her eyes that were asking the question.

"Neil," she yelled, staring at her friend. "I got your text!"

"He's just popped out to the shops, he'll be back in a minute."

For a moment Nasra just held on to her friend, she couldn't speak. Then, moving her hands with urgency, she retrieved the mobile phone from her jacket pocket and started to scroll.

"But you told me ..." She didn't need to finish her sentence. Staring at the screen, it started to dawn on her what might have happened. Just the other day she had needed put her sim card into an old mobile device that she was now temporarily using as her smart phone kept freezing. Frantically her fingers scanned the keypad before coming to a sudden halt. She waited intently for a few seconds, then came the familiar sound of the message ring tone. *Could that be all it was?* Deleting old texts had freed up the memory. The rest of the message that she had been meant to receive earlier now came through and displayed on the screen . . .

"Neil is dead ... keen we all make up. We are good now. Come over and we can talk. J."

Nasra gathered her thoughts as Judy patiently awaited an explanation for the overreaction.

"My God, I only got the first three words of your text ... this crappy old phone." Nasra held the screen up so Judy could see. Judy put her hand to her mouth and gasped, now understanding some of what Nasra must have just gone through.

The two walked into the front room, Nasra took off her coat

and sat down, still in a state of shock. Could she really tell her friend the rest of what she had just experienced?

"I'll make us a cup of tea" Judy moved into the kitchen, raising her voice slightly in order to continue the conversation.

"Yeah, Neil came back a couple of hours ago. We had a chat about all sorts of stuff and we are okay now." The sound of water filling a kettle broke the dialogue, then Judy walked to the doorway with the kettle in her hand. "Look, anyway, I'm sorry. I shouldn't have stormed off like that. I'm glad you've come round."

Nasra smiled at her friend. It had been a long day.

✿ ✿ ✿ ✿ ✿

The events of that day haunted Nasra. For the next few weeks she couldn't get it out of her mind. Had she really picked up Neil and taken him on some perilous journey out of town? Or had she had some sort of mental melt down on the way? The blur between dreams and reality was swelling and sometimes nothing seemed to make sense. Nothing that is, until she found herself doing some research.

Every evening when she got home she would find herself thinking deep and asking questions as she sat alone. Her jigsaw of the city, past and present still lay on the table, incomplete, books were still scattered around her cluttered living room unread, but she had spent a lot of time on her computer researching local history. There was something about the past that was starting to fascinate her: the tales Neil had told, the story behind her bracelet, and even the old necklace that seemed to have its own role to play. As with most things in life, the deeper you look, the more you discover. This was the case for Nasra over the passing weeks.

13. Dreams of the Past

Peterborough: Late August, 2014

The days passed as summer rolled on. For all three of them
– Neil, Judy and Nasra – what happened next was to shape
the rest of their lives. We never know what's around that next
corner, what card life might deal us next. What happened
wasn't anything that the three of them were expecting.

The end of the month loomed closer and Neil and Judy felt
the end of summer too. The temperature of late had been much
cooler and the evenings were drawing in. It wouldn't be long
now until their new arrival.

It was a Friday afternoon while Judy was hanging out her
washing when she decided she needed a change of scenery.
Her swelling womb was ready to drop, the days were long
while Neil was at work, and she just needed some company.
She knew her friend had a long weekend booked and she
hadn't spoken of any particular plans so she gave her a call.

It was a fine day, and if the truth be known, Nasra
Chowdhury was at a loose end too, and so when Judy called,
she was happy to pop over.

❖ ❖ ❖ ❖ ❖

The two women sat talking over a cup of tea in the garden
of the Presslands' home. They talked about this and that: how
Judy had been feeling in these final weeks before birth, how

excited they were about the arrival of the baby, and how Neil was keeping. Then, Nasra found herself talking about other stuff, and Judy listened to her friend intently. She listened not only to the details Nasra told of the dream she kept having, but also of what she'd done by way of research. What Nasra told her friend that night would remain with her most probably forever.

"I keep finding myself in all sorts of mixed up situations, in much the way that dreams generally go, you know? But there's always a problem – a desperate task or a moment of imminent danger. I seem to solve it, but never know how! Someone will turn up at the end and congratulate me." Nasra paused.

"Congratulate you?"

"Yes, just with unsubstantial comments like: '*I told you so*' or '*Mark my words my dear*' or sometimes just a beaming smile and saying something like '*You've done very well . . . until next time . . .*' It's always very mixed up."

Judy sipped her tea. She was interested, but we all dream strange things from time to time. Nasra went on to explain how one morning she had awoken feeling absolutely sure she'd just been walking in a woods gathering plants or herbs or something like. As she woke up there was a voice telling her that what she had experienced in her dream had all happened centuries ago in another time – another world, and yet it had seemed so real! Almost as soon as she was deeply disturbed by the powerful impression left by the dream, she would forget all the precise details.

Judy was partially interested, but this was just a dream. She neither understood nor possessed the intellect to try and work out any of this *clever meanings* stuff for herself, but what did get her full attention was what her friend told her of some of the things she'd discovered by way of research. In fact, she found this quite startling:

"I've been researching online. It's amazing what you can find out if you dig deep."

"Oh? What have you been researching?"

"Just about some of Peterborough's past. The City has quite a history." Nasra paused briefly to drink her tea.

"Did you know that the Cathedral was once the Abbey, inhabited by monks right back from the first millennium? A weird thing I came across were these stories about ghostly monks who have appeared to people all around the Cathedral over time." Nasra paused as if expecting her friend to say something but Judy's eyes just widened slightly as she took in the words. Nasra continued:

"I know Neil said he saw something in the grounds – the figure dressed as a monk, Remember?"

"Oh yes, but come on, that was the day of the festival, we all know how much was going on that day."

"Yes, but your dearly beloved went to great lengths to point out *where* he met the chap ... don't you remember ... in the Cathedral grounds?"

Judy felt a mental jolt, her mind started working faster. Hadn't Neil reacted rather strangely? This single event had certainly affected him.

"And, something else I found out," continued Nasra. "Back in the fourteen hundreds there is a story about a group of young monks who got fed up with their simple monastic life. They went out on a rampage and returned to the Abbey one night in a heavily drunken state. They were sent out to the countryside, to the Grange out on Oxney road towards Eye, as a punishment. When they got there apparently it all just cooked up some more. The supervising monk in charge was taken ill and they were left to their own devices. Guess what happened? They carried on and did it all again ... this time getting completely drunk! And, at least one of them ended up getting killed in some sort of brawl!"

Judy felt a cold tingle, that feeling you might get when perhaps the pieces of a complex jigsaw seem to be falling unexpectedly into place. She stood up.

"I'm getting cold." She said, walking slowly back towards the house, indicating for Nasra to do the same. Her body language told her friend that some piece of that slightly uncomfortable jigsaw *had* just fallen into place in Judy's mind right then and there. Judy put her cup on the kitchen table and placed her hands on the back of the chair for support.

"He got drunk one night a few months ago, him and his mates – they all did. And, he said it was like something big looming over him."

"I'm sorry, what?" Nasra didn't understand this last remark.

"Like it was watching him – in his dreams ..." Judy turned suddenly to face her friend. "Remember I think I told you before, he said he felt it *was* actually the Cathedral! – this thing in his dream!" Nasra was beginning to understand. Somehow, Neil felt threatened and insecure, and the Cathedral seemed to be the key.

She thought of her own dreams too. They were like a message from the past but they seemed so real at the time. She clasped her hands together then released them, allowing her fingers to spring free.

Then, as her fingers subconsciously touched inside her sleeve to scratch her wrist, Nasra felt the hard smooth metallic surface of her bracelet, and immediately she remembered Eileen O'Darcy giving it to her all those weeks ago. She had taken to wearing it more or less ever since that day as it seemed to make her feel, well, just good in some way or other. Judy noted her nervous actions.

"You like that thing, don't you." Judy smiled, she didn't intend to sound patronising.

"Yes, do you like it?" Nasra rolled back her sleeve to display it to her friend, pleased to change the subject.

"I love those gems around the plate." Judy pointed to the intricately decorated silver panel that looked as if it perhaps should hold a tiny inscription of some kind. "Is there any mark?"

"No there isn't. I did think ... but no, silly idea."

"What?" Judy grinned.

"I was going to say it should say something like ... I don't know ... like something related to good fortune in some way." Judy scrutinised her friend's dreamy gaze.

"Like 'Good luck where ever you go'?" (Now her friend was being patronising.)

Nasra threw her friend a sheepish glance.

"It just feels ... I don't know ... sort of good ... like lucky – when I'm wearing it."

"Which is virtually all the time," chirped Judy, now with her tongue in cheek.

The two friends laughed. Judy looked at the clock on the living room wall and Nasra followed her gaze.

"Neil will be home soon, better get tea started."

"I'd better be making tracks too," Nasra said.

The two women rose to their feet.

14. Neil in Trouble

Later that evening, as they sat together on the sofa in front of the television, Judy decided to tell Neil about her friend's strange experiences and what she'd found out by way of research. Had she really thought this through? If she had, then perhaps she shouldn't have been alarmed by her husband's reaction. When confronted with mystery we all like to try to put the pieces of the jigsaw together; Judy was no exception.

"I had to tell you. Crazy isn't it?"

Neil murmured an acknowledgement, looking straight past Judy and out through the window.

"You wouldn't want me not to have told you." Judy tried to smile, but her husband's reactions were making it difficult.

"No, but I just feel now I need to know more."

"Well, I'm only saying what Nasra told me," replied Judy, a little crestfallen.

"Yeah, but it's like ... only half the story." Judy was puzzled.

At that moment Neil's phone buzzed, he pulled it from his pocket. Staring at the screen for just a moment he quickly pressed a couple of buttons then put it away. Judy clocked his body language, something wasn't right, he seemed so very tense. Why couldn't he just relax? *I suppose it's to be expected.* She thought, patting her bulge and smiling across at him.

"Come on," she said, sliding closer to him, "let's have an early night, we can talk in bed."

Neil, turned his head to face her with furrows across his forehead and his eyes squinted.

"I've got things to do, it's only just gone nine!"

"Up to you then, but I'm going to watch a bit of TV in the bedroom. I've had a few aches and pains today. Come up when you're done." Judy smiled, gave her other half a peck on the cheek then left him to ponder over things.

Five minutes later Neil's phone vibrated once more. He stared at it for just a few seconds before frantically running his fingers over the keypad with one hand as he rose to his feet, grabbing his jacket from the hallway bannister with the other. He called up to Judy saying that he was going out for a bit. The sound of her reply contained just a tinge of anxiety, but at that moment it was lost on Neil.

It was a stressful time, the baby's arrival was imminent, and Judy felt her partner's mind was not fully in gear and ready for the change their lives were about to experience. Now, he'd gone out again. This had been a regular occurrence all through the summer. How long he would be this time was anyone's guess! Hadn't he said that some of his mates were going to the football match this evening?

Shuffling herself back against the pillow in an effort to get more comfortable, she stopped still as another thought entered her head. What if he meets up with them afterwards and comes back stupidly late? She found herself recalling the last time he'd gone out for an evening on the spur of the moment and how it had led to a late night drunken parade through the Cathedral precincts. Turning to her right she could see the bedside clock; twenty past nine — might be hours before he's back.

Suddenly she wasn't tired at all, but bothered by something she couldn't put her finger on exactly. All that had actually happened was she was having an early night and Neil had decided to go out. What was wrong with that? Well, what was wrong was that Judy really didn't want to be alone right now, she felt very on edge and she needed to not be alone. She texted her friend, and when she cried 'lonely' Nasra was more than happy to come back over and keep her company for the rest of the evening.

Judy rang her husband's mobile but it rang out with no reply. She sent him a text and waited a minute or two, but there was no reply to that either. This actually made things worse in Judy's mind. Why wouldn't he answer?

Nasra could see that her friend was worried, he could at least have told her when he would be back.

"Perhaps he's just talking to someone. Relax girl, it's not the end of the world."

"I don't know. I just don't know why he's done this." Judy ran both hands over her forehead and through her hair. She tried his mobile again – still no reply.

"Have you *any* clue as to where he has gone?"

"No. I'm going to text his mates, someone might know, or at least have some clue where he is."

For the next few minutes the texts were flying between

folks they both knew who might have some knowledge of where he was. At first Nasra felt Judy should have just waited and not let herself get so worried about it, but as each message reply drew a blank, Judy's state of mind became worse. Ten minutes later they got a reply from one of his mates saying that he had talked about a barbecue ... somewhere in Fletton. It was definitely happening tonight. His mate Paddy had received a text saying he would *'b there in 10!'*

Five minutes later the girls were on the road heading southwards from Bretton towards Fletton. Judy had rushed to make herself ready and was quite uncomfortable but she needed to know where her husband was and what he was doing. Fletton was only a ten minute journey.

❖ ❖ ❖ ❖ ❖

He leaned his head forward as much as he practically could. It was a strain to hear what the guy was saying the music was so loud. As Neil sipped his can of lager he could tell that this occasional acquaintance that stood before him was no happy individual right now. Not all of his words had been clear, he had been here for an hour or two now and probably seen off several beers, but Neil was getting the picture. Clearly something he'd mentioned to the guy months ago, perhaps with more clarity than he'd cared to remember, was coming back to haunt him. He'd had to come and meet up, it would have been a bad move to ignore this guy and avoid facing the music.

"Okay mate. I get what you're asking but there's a problem." Neil was attempting something of an explanation but it wasn't going well. The guy's glazed steel grey eyes were fixed firmly upon his subject. He was *not* happy with what he was hearing.

❈ ❈ ❈ ❈ ❈

Minutes later the Micra pulled up outside a house in Fletton High Street. Nasra glanced across the road towards another house she new well, just off the street in a side road. *This must be the place she was on about weeks ago*, she thought. How different the area looked now on this late summer evening. They knew they had the right place, they could tell from the loud drone of a heavy bass beat coming from the property. As they clambered out of the car and could see that the side gate to the property was slightly ajar. Cautiously the two women made their way towards it and peered through the open crack. Right away they could see Neil was sitting there, talking to someone across the garden, Judy tried to get his attention.

"We might have to just get ourselves in there," whispered Nasra. Her friend pursed her lips, the lines across her forehead betrayed her weariness. This wasn't the type of place she had envisaged, and it was certainly not somewhere she wanted to be in her heavily pregnant state. She sensed that the next few minutes may prove to be an uncomfortable experience. Scanning the immediate vicinity through the twenty-centimetre gap the open gate afforded her, she quickly got the picture.

This was some rowdy gathering, where nobody seemed to have much regard for the noise levels they were creating, the mess they were making or the effect it might be having on the neighbours or anyone else for that matter. If they stepped inside, it might then be difficult to get away, but surely they would have to? Unless she could find him first and entice him away. But how were they going to do that? Them being there was probably the last thing he would expect to see. It was a bit like a time a few months ago when she had arrived round at her mum's house to be met by an old schoolfriend who had met up with her mum in the street and tagged along back to the house because she knew Judy would be arriving there to visit shortly – it kind of throws you when it's unexpected. The choices were stark, but she had already made up her mind that she didn't want to join this party.

At that moment, Neil's eyes met theirs through the gap in the gate. Was he glad to see them, or was he embarrassed to see his wife and her friend discovering him right there and then? Either way, he instinctively beckoned them over and seconds later Judy and her friend found themselves standing beside him right in the thick of things. The other guy took little notice of the pleasantries of introduction as he continued the conversation he was having with Neil, not at all concerned that he had an audience.

"Are you telling me you haven't got it? I've been waiting. You said you'd sell – been trying to get hold of you, but you don't reply bud – not good."

Neil shuffled around on his seat and rubbed his hand on the back of his neck as he glanced up at the two women. Judy was already feeling very uncomfortable. Was it the case that he had apparently, several months earlier during a previous alcohol-fuelled jaunt, promised something to this guy? Judy and Nasra were quickly getting the picture; he'd promised to sell him *the necklace!* It had started back in June and was meant to happen as soon as this mate had the means to pay him. The guy had been texting and Neil had been ignoring him.

Nasra noticed something else: Neil was wearing his football scarf. Her automatic reaction was then to look around to see that so too were a group of other guys who had just arrived. Of course! The new season was just round the corner and local team, the POSH, had played their first home game on this late August evening. Neil had intended to go, but this was more important to him and he had changed his mind.

"I want that necklace, man." The guy sounded quite animated. "Now you said it was as good as mine if I had the cash. I rocked up that day ... remember ... back in the summer when we were supposed to meet?"

Just then came an awkward and unpleasant interruption. Raised voices from across the garden stopped all of them in their tracks. A well-muscled man in a black t-shirt was shouting in the face of a girl, and they quickly acquired an audience as the poor girl was verbally humiliated. Others looked on as it swiftly escalated to a violent level. The guy in the t-shirt reached out and slapped the girl square in the face. Immediately two guys nearby pulled him away and a scuffle broke out before he was suitably restrained. Another woman went to the aid of the girl in distress. What really sickened Judy was the grin on the face of the guy her husband was at loggerheads with, it was as if he'd just enjoyed seeing the violently uncomfortable episode unfold before him. She felt a pain in her stomach and wanted them all to just get away from the ugly environment.

Nasra's heart was pounding and her brain started darting from one random thought to another. Her mind was at battle with itself trying to relate what she had just seen to what she was seeing in front of her, and to things that had already happened around her. Unconsciously, she clenched her fist slightly, and when she did so she once again became aware of the bracelet. Then, another thought popped into her head; she realised how close they were to where she'd first found that bracelet, between the crack in a floorboard in dear old Eileen's house just around the corner from where she now stood.

How strange that was. Next, the sound of a breaking glass

triggered the uprising of more testosterone-fuelled vocal cries from another part of the garden. Someone had sent a drink flying; now it was getting ugly.

Neil, having said very little to this point, felt Judy's hand grab his, and he immediately felt the fear flowing through her ... and into him. A big guy standing a few feet away, quite animatedly grabbed each end of his scarf as if in anticipation of something.

Nasra felt sick feeling in the pit of her stomach, something else had just clicked in her mind, and another piece of that uncomfortable jigsaw was falling into place: The bracelet – it made her feel good, but things that hang around the neck – there was something bad about them. Nasra instantly then remembered the necklace and how Neil told them he had given it to the strange character he'd met near the Cathedral that day back in June.

"Come on, let's go," whispered Judy, hoping Neil would hear. The guy's eyes were still firmly fixed on her husband's in spite of the distractions now springing up all around them. As the guy's attention was momentarily diverted towards a fresh dispute emanating from the other side of the garden, Neil seized the moment and quickly rose from his seat.

Then, just for a second or two, that strange event from a few weeks earlier when Neil had appeared differently to her haunted Nasra. *That car journey!* She thought as she set her gaze upon her friend, as if expecting to see something different about him. As she stared she noticed his scarf, and suddenly, in a flash, those signs burned an imprint on her brain . . . bracelet – good ... necklace – bad! Everything happened so quickly. A guy was stretching his scarf, wrapping each end around his hands as if about to use it around someone's neck! Neil's scarf hung loose from *his* neck as the three of them made their getaway from the angry would-be scarf collector. Two blokes were now at each other and one was having his scarf pulled from him. Somebody tried to grab Neil's scarf as the three of them scrambled towards the gate, but Nasra forced herself between the stranger and her friend. This was a dangerous but necessary action to take she told herself. Her own heart was pounding now, they had to get out of this place ... and quickly!

"Just get us out of here." Judy's desperate breathless tone came out almost as a shriek. Her bulging stomach now ached and a cool, clammy, unpleasant sensation came over her.

"Through here, quick." Nasra took control, bustling her friends through the gateway that wouldn't budge any further than half way as the base of its frame jarred against the paving slabs. Once through they made their way urgently along the path back to Nasra's car.

Nasra reversed the Micra out of the roadside parking space as her friends glanced nervously back towards the half open gateway. It didn't look as if anybody had reacted to their sudden departure. Seconds later, Nasra realised she was once again in a car with Neil, driving hurriedly through the streets of Peterborough, but this time it was to lead them all to a very different outcome. They had hardly travelled away from Fletton before the next chapter in this chain of events was to unleash itself.

Judy was in obvious discomfort. Were the events of the evening to prove too much for her laden state? Her body was telling her it was time.

"Neil," she gripped his hand.

"What is it? Judy. Are you in pain?"

"Neil, I think they're starting."

Nasra Chowdhury's mind was fully focused on a safe getaway, she couldn't sense the urgency of the conversation springing up from the back of her car. After glancing in her rear view mirror almost continually for the first half mile or so she was now happy that they weren't being followed. Her brain was trying to tune back into the strange significance of the moment: Arguments, a rowdy scene, testosterone getting the better of many men, neckwear being used in anger ... and those dreams ... there was something else as well. What was it trying to push it's way to the front of her mind? She looked ahead ... *The Cathedral!* Always it seemed they were drawn towards it, or at least, events seemed to involve it. It was as if it had some place in everything that was happening around them – like it held some special power. Now it was beginning to make sense, Nasra was on the cusp of understanding what everything meant, but her concentration was then to be diverted.

"Nasra, hospital." Neil's commanding voice came loudly and urgently from the back of the car. "She's having contractions, it's starting – the baby is coming!"

"Oh my God!" Yelled Nasra. "Okay, don't worry, I'll get you to hospital."

This was really going to happen now. Nasra, shaken back to the moment of present reality calculated the quickest route to take as Neil dug for his mobile. They were not far away at all.

Brightness flickered all around as once again the lights

seemed to hypnotise her. Right at this very moment she got that feeling that everything happening around *was* the important message – just for her! *Neil,* she thought, *he is key to everything that's happened* ... the jigsaw was nearly complete.

15. Full circle

The birth was straightforward. This might be considered as something of a surprise given their recent circumstances. Judy's labour was long, and Nasra had stayed with her friends until the early hours before deciding to go home and get what sleep she could.

When Nasra eventually got home and was able to find those critical few moments that we all need at the end of a momentous day, she found herself sitting on her sofa looking around her room. It was amazing. Neil and Judy were no longer two, they were a family of three. Her mind pictured the image of the tiny little baby, a boy, that had been born to them just two hours earlier. It was so wonderful, and right then Nasra felt so happy for them. Everything had turned out alright, but ... there was something else. Something was still nagging her, as if there was something she had to do in spite of everything that had happened that day. Kicking off her shoes and stretching her legs, she got up from the sofa and walked across the room to the jigsaw that was still laid out on the table, still not quite complete. Suddenly, she felt a mildly sharp sensation piercing her foot, she looked down. *Another bloody piece caught in the pile of the rug,* she thought. She picked it up. *I'm too tired for this – just need to get to bed.* But then, she found herself drawn towards the table, towards the jigsaw ... and towards the image of the Cathedral. Turning it in her hand as she studied it, and then the picture that was almost complete, surely, this was the final piece of her jigsaw!

❄ ❄ ❄ ❄ ❄

It was the next evening, and yesterday now seemed so long ago. So often this is the effect that such a huge event has on one's sense of time. Things can seem as if they happened so much longer ago, but, actually, everything has its place in time. Nasra had only managed to grab a few hours sleep earlier that morning but she needed to be there with her friends.

Judy sat up in her hospital bed with her husband at one side and best friend the other, proudly gazing across at the tiny little baby boy that had entered their world in the early hours.

"I told you," she grinned at Neil who looked puzzled, "told you it would be a summer baby."

They hadn't realised at this point, but he was actually two and a half weeks early; today, 27th August, was still summer.

Judy was tired, so once she'd nodded off and the little one was under the watchful eye of the staff nurses, Neil and Nasra made their way downstairs for a coffee.

"I feel so odd!" declared Neil after his first sip of the hot liquid.

"It's to be expected, you two have been through so much. It must feel wonderful though."

"Of course, yeah it does, but it hasn't really sunk in yet." He looked across at Nasra, placing his cup firmly on the table. "You've been through a lot with us as well you know. We do appreciate your support." Nasra smiled. "Anyway, I wanted to catch up with you about all that historical research stuff you were doing."

Nasra raised her eyebrows and threw him a grin, this one of mild surprise.

"You really want to talk about all that now?"

Neil did, and, if the truth be known, so did Nasra. So they talked, and she told him all about the events of hundreds of years earlier that were supposed to have taken place. For the first time Neil could see a parallel with not only himself, but in the dreams he'd had too. There was the secondary knowledge he seemed to have about certain things, the stories he'd told about the experiences he'd had. But why? What did it all mean?

What Nasra told him was that they were all signs – like cryptic replays from the past, sent to guide them. Now, she could see it all; Neil had been in danger last night, but somehow she saw in him someone else – someone who *wasn't* Neil. She had been given a reward because she performed an act of kindness for an old lady, this had made her feel good, and now good things had happened. The necklace however ... that had brought nothing but bad luck. Now Nasra knew why:

"The events all those years ago ... back in the fourteen hundreds ... they are repeating in our lives right now. I've had dreams too, and sometimes, just sometimes ..." Nasra stumbled with her words, but Neil didn't interrupt, he knew that what she was trying to say was important. "Sometimes it's as if I was really there, as if somehow I have some control over events back then ... and now. What we are doing right now is real."

Nasra looked Neil hard in the eyes grasping his hand as he hung on to every word she was speaking; "Ever heard the phrase, *The truth is stranger than fiction?*" she asked of him. He didn't need to answer her, they were living the truth right now, and frankly, you couldn't make it up! Neil just smiled back at her.

"Come on, let's go and see how Judy's doing."

"So where did all this come from?" Judy, in spite of everything that had happened over the last few weeks, and, understandably as she had just given birth, was still rather puzzled. Neil and Nasra had told her what they knew and why they both now felt it was important, but Judy wasn't getting it. So as Judy asked the question, both she and Neil turned their attention to their friend – the person they felt sure could now clarify things.

So, Nasra began to explain to them what she felt; how some things in life seem that they were just meant to happen, as if it was obvious for us to follow a certain path. We don't always know why we do what we do, but if we are honest with ourselves we are instinctive creatures and we read the signs, follow the course, and draw conclusions from the experiences we gain.

As Nasra went back over all the events of the summer that had befallen them they could relate it to the process of completing a jigsaw; some parts are easy and the process just flows, but then there's a piece you can't quite place and you find yourself out of your comfort zone. Different emotions get the better of you and sometimes you can even feel cheated, as if an impossible task has just been placed before you. Then, you suddenly find that last piece and you wonder what all the fuss was about.

"But, what I don't get is, how is that stupid necklace thing Neil used to wear is so significant?" Judy was interested, but was finding the discussion all a bit highbrow, she just wanted the obvious gaps to be filled in for her.

"It's because of you Judy. Don't you see? Think. Where and when did you and Neil first get together, I mean really start going out?" This wasn't really a question: Her friend scrutinised her gaze as Judy paused, collecting her thoughts. Then she started to remember.

"It was years ago ... that night ... after the fire out at that big old house on Eyebury Road, I found that necklace thing, and I gave it back to him."

Right then it became Judy's turn, her moment to place a piece of that jigsaw down on the table, as all at once certain things started to dawn on her.

"That necklace, it was like ... so old. It was from another time, Neil never should have had it!"

"Yes, that's right, and once it found its way home, things started to put themselves right," finished Nasra. "I think we have all been given a part to play, and, like any actor, there have been lines to learn, but we have been given some pretty smart prompts." Nasra continued to explain what she felt she now knew: "In the centre of this City is an ancient and splendid building, it seems we are never far away from it. Remember, you thought you saw Neil there? Who you really saw we will never know, but remember also, it was the centre of things for the folk of six hundred years ago; there was no escaping the power it held over the monks of the time, and it seems that things that happened to people then were very powerful moments in the history of this place. From time to time they have replayed as *ghostly visions*. We are experiencing a reflection of what really took place. Whatever the exact details were, whatever myths have suffered unsubstantiated embellishment over the span of time, what we are experiencing now is real!"

You could have heard a pin drop in that hospital room as Nasra continued:

"You see, what is time? What does six hundred odd years matter? We are still the same people, we have the same instincts, same experiences and we are here in the same place. It's a place in time. What happened then has affected us, and our presence here now has relevance to the past. Don't you feel it? I've been part of something from long ago, in my dreams ... I'm sure of it ... and I think you both have too."

Sometimes the truth *is* stranger than the fiction.

The conversation was becoming very deep. Judy looked across at her tiny little son as he turned his soft head from side to side, his eyes tightly closed. She looked at his perfect features, his tiny fingers, his downy hair. Neil clasped her hand. At that moment came a familiar voice:

"Hello dear." Judy's mum had arrived. "How are you both?" She grinned, giving her daughter a huge embrace before then going through the standard emotions of a grandmother seeing her grandson for the first time.

Once the emotional formalities were over, Grandmother Jenny asked what all mothers ask and assumed what mothers assume. She wanted to know his birth weight, and then, she said;

"So it's little Ryan then is it? Do you have a middle name for him or is it just going to be Ryan?"

Judy and Neil looked at each other. *Ryan* had been the

standard likely choice of name they had branded around, and it was being taken 'as read' by Judy's mum. Neil and Judy hadn't spoken about this for a while, but somehow, they both knew what the other was going to say:

"No, no, you see ..." Judy looked at her husband again, as if for reassurance before continuing;

"I had this dream last night ... didn't we." She turned to Neil who then took over:

"We both had the same dream." He smiled at Judy. Nasra stared at both of them savouring this sweet clear moment of anticipation.

"It's not Ryan," said Judy.

"It's Richard," blurted Neil, as his wife smiled and gripped his hand a little tighter before completing her son's name.

"Yes, Richard, Dominic, Pressland." Husband and wife smiled at each other.

Nasra Chowdhury smiled too; their jigsaw was now complete.

❊ ❊ ❊ ❊ ❊

Fact or Fiction?

The Facts:

Back in the mid fourteen hundreds when the Abbey existed on the site of where the Cathedral of Peterborough has now stood since it's completion in 1193, a group of young monks were sent out to Oxney Grange out at Eyebury, three miles to the north east of the city centre, as a punishment. They had gone for a night out, got very drunk and had become quite unruly. Once out at the Grange they were not properly supervised; the senior monk in charge had apparently been taken ill. Only infrequent check visits would ever have been undertaken by the Abbot who would most probably have turned up unannounced. This allowed them to continue their drunken antics. Some sort of brawl ended up with the death of at least one, and possibly two of the monks. This is documented to have taken place although the exact circumstantial facts remain unclear.

On August 27th 2003, Oxney Grange, the farm building that remained on the site of the original manor house was burned to the ground. The exact circumstances of how this happened remain unclear, but is thought quite possibly to have been arson. There had been a building remaining on the same site for six hundred years where it was originally owned by the Abbey as the rehabilitation home for trainee monks, as occurs in the story. During the nineteen eighties and nineties it became an old people's home. At the time of writing it has been developed into a closed community of plush expensive rented properties.

There are stories among local industrial workers of at least one factory in the Eastfield area of the city being haunted by a phantom who was once a worker there that apparently died in some tragic accident.

There are various documented accounts of 'ghostly monks' having been seen in and around the Cathedral of Peterborough.

The Peterborough festival has taken place in recent years covering various venues including the town park. All local areas and venues mentioned in the story are real places.

Reference to the Abbot, John Deeping and to the country being at a point of unrest during the mid fifteenth century, (reign of the boy king Henry VI), are correct.

The Author had the real experience as given in Nasra's account of remembering her father telling the story of a car hitting the central reservation. In the author's experience he feels it was incredibly fortunate that he made the decision to overtake the car when he did, and that the flow of traffic seemed to disappear during that precise minute, thus averting disaster.

It's Fiction:

All the characters, past and present, are fictional, and any perceived direct representation of anyone living is unintentional.

There are no records of a particular monk name of Richard, or any of the other named characters featured in this story from past or present.

There is nothing to suggest that there ever was an artefact of any type; bracelet, necklace or otherwise, discovered in or around the area, or that any such item was actually used as a murder weapon at any time in the past ... but then ... who knows! Sometimes the truth is stranger than the fiction!

❁ ❁ ❁ ❁ ❁

About The Author

Tom Goymour was born and raised in Cambridgeshire UK. and has lived in Peterborough for over forty years. He writes mainly in the mystery and suspense genre about what he sees, thinks, and instinctively feels.

Being part of a large family has given him many powerful experiences from which to draw inspiration. He is an exponent of art and design and a composer of piano music, but tries hard not to inflict any of this on others!

Empowered by his many, and sometimes strange experiences, he has found writing to be his voice-piece. He is a meticulous studier of life, and his stories nearly always contain a twist or a strong moral message that hits home hard . . . designed to make the reader think

Like what you've read?
Get the other books availablein this series.

Printed in Great Britain
by Amazon